A LION'S PRIDE

THE SERIES

When An Alpha Purrs

(A Lion's Pride, #1)

Eve Langlais

Copyright © April 2015, Eve Langlais
Cover Art by Yocla Designs © May 2015
Edited by Devin Govaere
Copy Edited by Pub-craft.com
Copy Edited by Amanda L. Pederick
Produced in Canada

Published by Eve Langlais
1606 Main Street, PO Box 151
Stittsville, Ontario, Canada, K2S1A3
http://www.EveLanglais.com

ISBN-13: 978 1927 459 775

Chapter One

"What do you mean Dominic isn't here?" Arik didn't quite raise his voice, and yet everyone in the barbershop heard him and noted his displeasure. Heads ducked, hands busied themselves snipping and styling, and no one dared meet his gaze.

If they were lion shifters, he would have said it was because they recognized his alpha status—say hello to the king of the concrete jungle. But these were only regular humans, people easily cowed by a man in an expensive suit with a commanding attitude.

Except for one.

"Granddad is out west."

The woman's reply had him spinning, and he inhaled sharply, which drew in more than just the scent of the barbershop. It drew in her tempting aroma—and stirred a hunger that had nothing to do with food.

Smells delicious. For a human.

Standing at just over five and a half feet, the woman barely reached his chin. She didn't let her shortness deter her. Her head tilted. The chin raised, almost defiantly, as she met his stare. Brown eyes framed in dark lashes didn't turn from his amber-hued ones.

Someone's got spirit. But he didn't have time to explore how far her attitude and bravery went. There were more important matters clamoring for his attention. Such as his poor, shaggy mane.

"What do you mean he's out west? I have an

appointment." People didn't cancel his appointments. Nor did they make him wait. The perks of being top of the heap.

"My Aunt Cecily had her baby early. He took some time off to go meet his new grandson."

A decent excuse, but still… "But what about my hair?" That might have emerged more plaintively than he'd like. However, who could blame him? They were talking about his precious luxurious mane that required a regular trim lest the ends grow ragged, or, worse, a split end dared to make an appearance.

Vanity, one of his faults, along with arrogance and an unwillingness to budge.

"No need to worry, big guy. I'm taking over Granddad's appointments while he's gone."

"You?" A girl, cut his hair? He couldn't help but laugh, the idea too ridiculous to contemplate.

"I'm sorry. I fail to see the entertainment."

"You can't seriously expect me to trust my mane to a woman?" Sexism, alive and well in Arik's world, the fault of the females in his pride who'd raised him. No coddling for Arik. They didn't believe in letting him play with dolls or caving to others. His mother and aunts, not to mention his numerous female cousins, had taught him to be tough. They didn't allow softness in his world, not when they groomed him as the future leader of their pride.

He was all male, all the time, and dammit, a man used a barber, not a hairdresser. Even if she was cute.

"Suit yourself. I've got more than enough men to take care of—"

Was that his cat growling?

"—without adding a pompous one to the list."

"Pompous?" Even if she'd pegged him right, it

didn't stop his indignant glare.

A glare she chose to ignore. She crossed her arms over her chest, plumping her cleavage—ooh, pretty, shadowy cleft. His curious nature drew his eyes to the mysterious and beckoning vee until she cleared her throat.

"My eyes are up here, big guy."

Caught. Good thing he was a cat. His kind had no shame, nor did they apologize. He shot her his most engaging, boyish grin. "My name is Arik. Arik Castiglione."

She didn't react to his smile or titles, so he elaborated, "The CEO for Castiglione Enterprises." He stretched his lips wide enough to engage his deadly dimple.

And still failed to impress.

She raised a brow. "Is that supposed to mean something?"

Surely she jested. Within his mind, his poor lion lay down in a traumatized heap and crossed its paws over its eyes.

"We are the largest importer of meat in the world."

Her shoulders lifted in a shrug. "I don't check the label to see who brings me my steak. I just eat it."

"What about our chain of restaurants? A Lion's Pride Steakhouses."

"Those I've heard of. Decent, I hear, but overpriced. I can get a bigger plate of food at LongHorn. And according to my girlfriends, the male waiters are cuter too."

For once, Arik found himself at a loss for words. His lion on the other hand? His mane was definitely ruffled—and itching.

Arik had already gone two weeks longer than

usual for this haircut because of an overseas business trip. Time to get back to his highest priority. "How long until Dominic is back?"

"A week, maybe two. I told him to take his time. Granddad doesn't often take time off, and he's getting up there in years."

A few weeks? He'd look like a wildebeest if he waited that long. "That's no good. I need a cut. Are there any male barbers available?"

"Afraid to let a girl touch your precious hair?" She smirked. "I can peek at the schedule and see if we can squeeze you in this afternoon."

"I don't have time to come back. I need it done now."

Usually when he used the word now, people jumped to do his bidding. She, on the other hand, shook her head.

"Not happening, unless you've changed your mind and are willing to let me cut it."

"You're a hairdresser."

"Exactly."

"I want a barber."

"Same thing."

Said the girl without a Y chromosome. "I think I'll wait."

Arik turned away from her, only to freeze as she muttered, "Pussy."

If she only knew how right she was. But, of course, she didn't mean the feline version.

Pride made him pivot back. "You know what. On second thought, you may cut my hair."

"How gracious of you, Your Majesty." She sketched him a mock bow.

Not funny, even if accurate. He glared in reply.

"I see someone's too uptight for a sense of humor."

"I greatly enjoy comedy, when I hear it."

"Sorry if my brand of sarcasm is too simple for you to understand, big guy. Now, if you're done, sit down so we can get this over with and send you and your precious hair back to your office."

A woman giving him orders? Not uncommon when a male lived surrounded by them. But actually obeying, that was new – and in this case, unavoidable.

Head held regally high, Arik took the proffered seat, putting his back to the female, but he could still watch her in the mirror and track her by scent. Coconut lotion, fabric softener, and musky woman. All woman.

My woman. Want to taste.

His lion grumbled in hunger. Odd because Arik had eaten a hearty breakfast, even wrestling his beta, Hayder, for the last two pieces of bacon.

The hairdresser swirled a fabric cape around his upper body, swathing him in protection against snipped tickly bits. So far the same as usual, except Dominic's mere presence never had Arik's body so aware. The light touch of her fingers at his nape as she fastened the Velcro closure caused all the hairs on his body to stiffen. And they weren't the only thing standing at attention.

Before he could wonder at his reaction, she withdrew her hand and busied herself with her tray of instruments. Razor, scissors, brush, comb. But forget the manly black colors a barber would use. Her tools were pink and black, zebra striped.

The indignity of it. He almost said something but held his tongue, only because he could see her watching and waiting for it in the mirror. As if he'd give her the satisfaction. This cat held his own tongue—for now.

The hairdresser sifted her fingers through his long strands, lifting and studying the various layers Dominic usually cut into it. Unlike many businessmen, Arik preferred to keep his golden mane somewhat long. Funny how many of his lovers had told him it gave him a leonine appearance—if only they knew the truth.

"How much are we taking off?"

As little as possible, given he still didn't trust her. "About a half inch or so. Just even up the ends." That should tide him over until Dominic returned.

"Are you sure?" She frowned at his crown, as she held long strands up. "You look like you could use at least two inches off, if not more."

How did she know? Arik usually kept his mane to a civilized length that just touched the top of his collar.

"I'm sure."

"You know, a man your age really should have a more mature cut. The shaggy surfer style is more suited to young guys."

He dug his fingers into the armrest and fought not to growl. "I like my hair like this."

"Suit yourself. I was just saying you'd look better with a shorter cut."

Shave his precious mane? Never! "Do you always argue with your clients?"

Her eyes met his in the mirror, and he wasn't surprised to see a smile lurking at the corners of her lips. "Only when they're wrong."

That surprised a bark of laughter from him. Despite his irritation with the situation, and her outspoken nature, he grudgingly liked Dominic's granddaughter. "Very well. You may cut it a little shorter than a half inch. But not much shorter. I do not want to end up scalped."

"For a man your age and in your position, you are way too obsessed with your hair," she muttered as she bound sections of his mane with hairclips. Not exactly his most manly look.

Arik kept a close watch for anyone with a camera or cell phone. Dare to take a pic and he'd probably go furry.

Okay, he wouldn't go furry in public, but he sure as hell would extract retribution. CEOs of billion-dollar corporations had an image to maintain, and pink hair clips holding his hair at crazy angles didn't exactly fit it.

"How come I've never met you before?" Dominic had paraded a great number of his children and grandchildren through his barber shop over the years.

Attention focused on her hands, which wielded a set of scissors, she answered. "I don't visit often. I live out in the Midwest with my mom and dad. I was actually working at a hair salon out there until it shut down, and Granddad offered me a job here."

"You just packed up and moved?"

"Why not?" She released a layer of hair, and the scissors kept snipping. Golden bits flittered to the floor, and Arik tried to not tense. There was just as much hair strewn as when Dominic cut it. She seemed to know her business when it came to using scissors, but for some reason, he couldn't shake his unease.

"Women should stay close to family." His female family members certainly did, despite his best efforts to pawn them off onto other tribes and cities. Hell, he'd even tried to bribe some of his more rascally cousins with the promise of condos on other continents. However, the lionesses in his pride were content. A sign he was a good leader, but annoying as it meant they were constantly putting their whiskered noses in his business.

And they also loved to play matchmaker.

"When are you going to give us some cubs?" Not a day went by that he didn't hear this.

"I've got a friend I want you to meet." Fun for a night, until the next day when his cousin hammered him to make some kind of commitment.

The hairdresser reacted to his statement about a woman's place with a snort. "Get with the times, big guy. We're no longer strapped to a kitchen or forced into arranged marriages. We even get to vote. Girls nowadays often move away from home and have jobs. Or at least this one does."

He couldn't help but wince as she gave a decisive snip to his mane. So far, everything looked good. Yet he could have sworn ominous music hummed at the edges of his mind, feeding a certain dread he'd never admit aloud.

Scared of this woman and her scissors? Never. And his lion reinforced this with a very masculine *rawr*.

Still though, she'd essentially accused him of being a chauvinist. He explained himself. "I did not mean to sound misogynistic. I merely stated that women often find comfort in having family around them."

"I do have family here."

"Touché." Then he couldn't have said what prompted him to ask, "What of your boyfriend? I'm sure he's not pleased at your abrupt departure."

She paused and stared at him in the mirror. "Is this your not-so-subtle way of asking if I'm single?"

"Was I being subtle? Let me rephrase then. Do you have a lover?" He'd challenge him to a duel if she did and—

Hold on a second. He wasn't challenging anyone, especially not the human boyfriend of a hairdresser he'd just met.

Just met, and yet wanted.

The realization made him frown. Time to hit the dating circuit again if a plump and mouthy human girl was capable of making him irrational. It didn't help that his lion urged him to rub against her and mark her with their scent—to keep other males away.

Not happening. Marking any kind of female was bound to create complications. Arik wasn't about to settle down or commit himself. He was in his prime. Playing the field.

Flirting with a hairdresser who set his hairs on end—and brought his erotic senses alive.

The things I could do to her. Nibbles on her creamy skin... Nips at that luscious lower lip, which pulled taut as she frowned at him and said, "First off, I don't think my love life is any of your business." Snip. "Second. Even if I were single, I wouldn't date you." Snip. Snip.

"Why not?" He could have blinked in astonishment when the query emerged from his mouth. However, a curious kitty needed to know. Women just didn't say no. It wasn't arrogant of him to claim it, not when it was fact.

Rejection was not something he encountered. Until now.

"Are you seriously having to ask why I won't date you?" She sounded so incredulous. "Would you like me to recite the list alphabetically?"

Actually, he did. "Let's hear it."

Not even a pause. "Asshat. Braggart. Cocky tied with chauvinist. Dumbass. Egotistical. Do I really need to go on?"

A chuckle rumbled forth from him—again. What was it about this woman that delighted him? She kept arguing and defying him at every turn, and yet he couldn't help but find her amusing. She utterly intrigued him, especially as he tried to guess what she'd say next. How refreshing to come across a female that wasn't related to him, or impressed by him, who dared to treat him as a man.

One she considered beneath her standards.

"I think your list needs tweaking." He launched a defense of his character.

"Oh really? And just how do you see yourself? I'm sure this will be good."

"Let me see. Attractive, bold, courageous, daring, elegant, ferocious, especially as a lover," he admitted with a wink. "Gallant."

With a derisive snort, she interrupted. "Ha. I highly doubt that."

"And yet you don't really know me. My lady friends would tell you that I am a gentleman." When it came to opening doors and picking up the check. Other than that, there was nothing gentle about him. Just ask those who crossed him.

Kings didn't let anyone question their authority.

"I wouldn't know, though, about this supposed gallantry, because I'm not your lady friend."

"You could be." He gave her another chance. She truly did draw him in with the roundness of her figure, hugged by faded denim and topped with a baggy sweatshirt that drooped enticingly off a shoulder, baring a black strap.

Lace or cotton? A feline mind wanted to know.

But apparently he wouldn't know today, as she, yet again, managed to resist him.

"Date you? Not likely."

Again words emerged from him without volition. "Why not?"

"Oh please. I've seen enough to know you're not my type."

Such a liar. Apparently he wasn't the only one aroused by their repartee. The musky scent of her arousal tickled his senses. It made him bolder. "I guarantee when I'm between your thighs and you're clawing my back, you'll be screaming a different tune."

So he might have come on a tad strong with that last statement. That was still no excuse for what happened next.

"Pig." However it wasn't the animal insult that was her most grievous crime. It was the gigantic hunk of hair she snipped off!

An irreplaceable, thick chunk of his hair permanently removed. Accidental or intentional, it didn't matter.

Ack! My mane. My beautiful, precious mane.

He couldn't help a low rumbling growl. His eyes glinted in the mirror, the gold catching the light and reflecting it, along with his fury.

"You. Did. Not. Just. Do. That." And yes, he might have growled the last bit.

"Oops? Did I do that? Sorry." Said with no repentance at all. With a smirk and a blown kiss, she let her crime rain down over him in a golden, threaded shower.

And then, she ran.

Chapter Two

"You. Did. Not. Just. Do. That." The client who'd blatantly sexually propositioned her sounded more beast than man. His evident rage and disbelief had her eyeing the clump of hair she had just hacked off.

Oh hell. I did not just do that. But she had. She'd cut the big guy's precious hair.

It's his own fault. Off balance since she'd met him, she blamed her raging hormones—which hadn't stopped turning giddy somersaults in her lower belly since she'd met him.

He'd walked in, and she'd gotten slammed with awareness. He spoke, and all her nerve endings tingled.

He also riled her like no man. She should hate him. Yet, instead, she wet her panties as she could so easily picture what he said.

Clawing, sweaty, hot sex.

With a guy who annoyed her and kept needling her until she snapped—and retaliated.

Treat me like a sex object indeed.

Later, she'd blame her hands for momentarily taking on a mind of their own and snipping.

At least for once, it wasn't her mouth getting her into trouble. However, instigating it didn't mean she'd stay to face the consequences. Not when the big guy looked fit to kill.

Listening to her sense of preservation, which screamed, "Run, you idiot!", Kira dropped her scissors and bolted.

Out the front door of the barbershop she streaked, barely noting the gaped mouths of the other patrons, as well as those of her uncle and cousin who also worked there.

The street noise proved varied and chaotic—engines humming, brakes screeching, voices chattering, the city teeming with life—but in spite of all this, she still heard the slam of a door hitting a wall, the chime of the bells strung on it, ringing in warning.

Even more worrisome was a bellowed, "Get your ass back here, woman!"

The imp in her, which apparently harbored a death wish, flashed him a finger.

Was that a roar? People around her didn't stumble or react, and yet she could have sworn she heard the echo of a lion in the phantom sound.

It only spurred her to run and dodge faster. By only the narrowest of margins did she manage to dart across the road just before a sluggish bus, with a stream of cars behind it, passed.

She used its bulky girth to cover her dash into the alley. Straight down, then through an open door, into a kitchen she knew well. Aunt Theona's pizza parlor.

It smelled so damned good. The yeast of freshly made dough, mixed with the tantalizing aroma of breadsticks cooking. If she wasn't in such a hurry, she would have stopped for a bite.

However, self-preservation kept her moving, leaping over the bucket on wheels full of sudsy water. She spun around the edge of the stainless steel counter and streaked past the hot ovens.

"Kira! What are you doing?" bellowed her

aunt, elbow deep in dough.

"Can't stop to talk. Running from an angry client," she shouted as she skipped through the swinging kitchen doors, weaved through the white Formica tables, and popped out onto another street, the market one. The throng of milling shoppers served as not only an effective 'Where's Kira?' camouflage, but meant too many witnesses for Mr. Big Shot to kill her.

Skipping through the people, Kira kept to the busiest spots until she hit the fish mart, owned by her uncle, Vince. In she popped, waving hi to him where he stood behind the counter. She headed straight to the storage room at the back. Inside the room, she took the stairs that led to the second floor and the apartment Uncle Vince had rented her when she moved out here a few weeks ago.

The perfect hideout.

A part of her couldn't help but mock her own cowardice in fleeing the irate businessman. However, she feared more by remaining and… what? Having him put her over his knee for a spanking?

Hmm. That might have been fun, especially if a kinky paddling led to something else.

Wrong.

So wrong.

How could she even be thinking such erotic things about the most arrogant jerk she'd ever had the misfortune to meet?

Probably because he was stupidly handsome.

Despite the fact his personality left a lot to be desired, she couldn't seem to stop an attraction to him. The asshole syndrome at work.

What was it about her that couldn't help craving the wrong guy?

Wasn't her last boyfriend lesson enough? He was, after all, the reason she'd come out here. To escape.

When will I ever learn?

With a sigh, she flopped onto her borrowed couch, the mismatched cushions a reminder of her messed-up life. The phone rang.

One glance at the call display and she grimaced. The hair shop. Probably her uncle calling to ask what the hell was going on. Kira didn't know what to tell him, so she didn't answer.

She knew her uncle wouldn't fire her, especially not once she told them what the big guy—*Arik, a name fit for a Viking in a romance novel*—had said to her. Heck, her cousins would probably form a lynch mob to confront him. Her family had an abundance of boys, and they tended to get rather protective of their sparse female cousins. A pity none of them lived in the Midwest close to her old home. She could have used them when she was having her problem.

But Arik hadn't yet done anything that merited their attention, and Kira had already handled the pompous businessman. No, she couldn't tell them what had happened, but she needed to talk to someone to cool her riled emotions, and she knew just who to call.

Number one on her speed dial. As the phone rang, she twirled a strand of hair around her finger.

"Kira, baby, what are you doing calling at this time? Shouldn't you be working?" Her mother answered, her voice immediately concerned. Who could blame her, given the events of the past few weeks?

"I was. But something happened." As she

relayed to her mother the events, a gush of words that ended with, "the nerve of that man," she expected commiseration.

Instead she got…laughter? "Oh my, but he sounds fascinating."

"Fascinating? You did hear the part where he sexually harassed me, right? Or what about the fact he's got caveman ideas? I mean come on, Mom. He claimed I wasn't good enough to cut his hair because I'm a girl."

"Oh please. As if that's something new. We both know that many men feel that way. Look at most of your cousins. And what about you? I know a certain young lady who insists on having only a certain aunt trim and color her hair."

Kira fidgeted. "That's different. Aunt Fiona is a master when it comes to highlights."

"Now who's being sexist?"

"You know I called you because you're supposed to be on my side."

"I am. Which is why I'm pointing out the obvious. You don't like this guy because he's assertive."

"Arrogant."

"Whatever. Yet we both know you need someone strong willed or you'll become bored."

"I'd say there's a lot to be said for boring. Especially since Gregory."

Eep. She'd said it aloud. He-who-should-not-be-named. A shiver went through her—as her ex probably walked over the grave he had planned for her—and she resisted an urge to yank the curtains to the apartment shut and check the lock on the door.

Her mother made a noise. "Grr. Don't talk to me about that man. He fooled us all, baby. But that doesn't mean every man is like him. There are good ones out there. Just look at your father and his brothers. Even your cousins. They would never hurt or disrespect a woman like that."

No, they wouldn't, but once punched, literally, often threatened, and her hair salon burned down in suspicious circumstances meant Kira was more than twice shy. She was mad, and scared, mostly because she feared the violence from her ex-boyfriend would spill over onto the ones she loved. "Well, it doesn't matter now. Even if the big guy was flirting and hinting at a date, I'm pretty sure he's changed his mind now after what I did to his precious hair."

After exchanging a few more tidbits of news, Kira hung up with her mother and let out a sigh. Here not even a week and already in trouble. With a man.

Could things get any worse?

Chapter Three

Things couldn't be any worse. Not only was a huge hunk of his hair missing from his precious mane, but Arik had lost her trail.

Him, a master hunter, evaded by a human.

His lion hung his head in shame.

It occurred to him, as he trudged back to the barbershop—with its striped spinning pole that always made him want to stop so his kitty could paw at it—that he should demand the folks working there cough up her address.

He could probably intimidate them into conceding. It didn't take much to have humans spill their guts, especially when he used his voice and stare on them. However, while he could easily snare her location, he'd lose his element of surprise, as they'd probably warn her.

He much preferred a sneak attack.

His steps bypassed the turn to the shop and, instead, headed to the rental parking lot that held his car.

Best to pretend he wouldn't retaliate. There was no benefit in rattling any cages for info, as it meant she would realize she'd gotten to him, that she'd managed to ruffle his fur.

Unacceptable.

Nothing fazed Arik. He was known as unflappable.

He was also wily. There were other ways to hunt a hiding mouse. Of course, before he could track her down via electronic methods, first he had to run the gauntlet at his office.

Did anyone dare say a word when he entered in his costly, Armani three-piece suit sporting a ball cap he bought from a street vendor, he who never wore a hat of any kind?

Curious gazes might have followed his path, but not a titter followed him. No one had big enough balls.

Except for Hayder, his second-in-command— the smartass—who trailed him into his office.

"Dude, what is up with the hat? When did you suddenly become a baseball fan?"

"I'd rather not discuss it," Arik said through tight lips and gritted teeth as his fingers tapped away, logging onto Facebook and doing a search on Dominic. Surely if the man had an account, it would be linked to his family members, including one feisty woman he needed to find.

To eat.

No. Angry or not, one didn't eat their enemy. It was uncivilized. And, yes, he intentionally misinterpreted his lion. He didn't even want to start thinking about the certain eating his other side had in mind.

There would be no cream lapping for her.

Or him.

Meowr. Such a disappointed sound.

A throat cleared. "Earth to Arik. Come in, boss."

With brows drawn, Arik glared at his beta. "What?"

"I was asking what had your boxers in a knot."

"You know I go commando."

"Usually, but something obviously has your

panties in a twist. Spill."

Oh, he spilled all right. Arik yanked off the hat and flung it against the wall and then swiveled his chair to get it over with.

Indrawn breath. A snicker. A full-on guffaw.

Arik swirled again and tossed deadly visual daggers at his second. "I fail to see the humor in my butchered mane."

"Dude. Have you seen it? It is bad. What did you do to piss Dominic off? Seduce one of his daughters?"

"Actually one of his granddaughters did this to me!" He couldn't help the incredulous note. The effrontery of the act still got to him.

A thump and a shake of the wall as Hayder hit it, his shoulders shaking with laughter. "A girl did that to you?" His beta convulsed with mirth, not at all daunted by Arik's glower and tapping fingers.

"This is not amusing."

"Oh, come on, dude. Of all the people to have a hair mishap, you are the worst."

"I look like an idiot."

"Only because you didn't let her finish hacking the rest off."

His fingers froze as he took his gaze off the screen for a moment to address the travesty. "Cut off my mane?" Was his beta delusional?

"Well, yeah. You know, to even it out so it doesn't show."

A growl rumbled forth, more beast than man, his lion not at all on board with any more trimming.

"Okay, if you're not keen on that, then what about a hair weave? Maybe we could get you a platinum one, or pink for contrast since you're being such a prissy princess about it."

That did it. A lion could take only so much. Arik dove over his desk and tackled his beta. Over they went with a thump and a tangle of limbs.

As he was slamming Hayder's head off the floor, snarling, "Take it back!" to his beta's chortled, "We'll get your nails done while they're weaving," Leo strode in.

A giant of a man, he didn't even have to strain as he grabbed them each by a shoulder and yanked them apart. But he didn't stop there. He slammed their heads together before shoving them down.

Arik and Hayder sat on the carpeted floor, nursing robin's eggs, united in their glare for the pride's omega, also known as the peacemaker. Of course, Leo's version of peace wasn't always gentle, which was why he was perfect for the pride.

The behemoth with the mellow outlook on life took a seat in a chair, which groaned ominously. "You do know that the staff two floors down can hear the pair of you acting like ill-behaved cubs."

"He started it!" Arik stabbed a finger at his beta. He had no problem assigning blame. Delegation was something an alpha did well.

Hayder didn't even deny his guilt. "I did. But can you blame me? He was pissing and moaning about this precious mane. All I did was offer a solution, and he took offense."

"I assume we're talking about the missing chunk of hair on our esteemed leader's head?" Leo shook his neatly trimmed dark crown. "I keep telling you that vanity is your weakness."

"And chocolate chip ice cream is yours. We all have our vices," Arik grumbled as he heaved himself off the floor and into his leather-padded seat—with built-in heating pad and massager because a man in his position did enjoy his luxuries.

"My vice is beautiful women," Hayder announced with a grin, adopting a lounging pose on the floor. Felines were king when it came to acting as if embarrassing positions weren't accidental at all.

"Don't talk to me about women right now. I'm still angry at the one who did this."

"I think I'm missing a key point," Leo stated.

It didn't take long to bring Leo up to speed. To his credit, the pride omega didn't laugh—long. "What are you planning to do?" Leo asked in a deep rumble.

"Do?" Good question. Arik couldn't beat the hairdresser. She was, after all, a girl. He couldn't eat her—she'd enjoy it too much—and he doubted he could get her to eat him—even if he would enjoy it very much. But, on the topic of eating, he could make her swallow her words... Wouldn't that be an awesome revenge?

"Uh-oh. Judging by the smile on his face, he just came up with a devious plan," Hayder announced. "Count me in if you need help."

Indeed, Arik had devised a perfect plan for revenge. In the game of cat and mouse, he was about to even the score.

Chapter Four

"Good morning, mouse."

The husky words just about had her wetting her pants. Leaving the key in the barbershop lock, Kira whirled around, so fast her coffee cup sloshed. Hot liquid splashed over her hand, and she yelped.

"Ouch!" She used the excuse of her burn to keep her attention focused on her hand instead of her unexpected visitor. A very tall visitor who'd obviously lain in wait for her.

Not good. Especially since, at this early hour, the sidewalks were still pretty bare.

Masculine fingers plucked the cup from her hand and tossed it at a nearby garbage bin. Before she could react, her injured appendage was raised, and he pressed his lips against her burning skin.

At the touch, her hand wasn't the only thing heating up.

Oh my god. She wanted to blame fear at the way her heart rate sped up, and for the slight tremor of her limbs, but she was old enough and experienced enough to recognize attraction.

"What are you doing?"

"Kissing it better." Except, he didn't stop at a simple kiss.

Kira tossed Arik a startled glance as he let the tip of his tongue lap at her coffee-burned skin, the touch raspier than expected. Nice. Too nice. She couldn't help but imagine that frictioning stroke against a more sensitive part of her body.

What the hell is wrong with me? Sanity reasserted itself, and she yanked her hand free.

"I don't need you making it better, especially since you're the reason I burned myself in the first place."

"Did I startle you, mouse?"

Her expression clearly said, *duh, what do you think.* He didn't seem repentant at all, judging by the smile curving his lips.

Ack. Look away. He was much too cute when he did that—and distracting. She tried to veer things back onto a less alluring footing. "What are you doing here?" As she asked, she cast a glance around for eye witnesses, anyone who might come to her aid should he decide to murder her for her faux pas of the day before.

Then again, perhaps she overreacted. He didn't seem angry today. On the contrary, his eyes smoldered with something, but if she wasn't mistaken, it was more like flirtation than ire.

Given his extreme reaction, and her recollection of his arrogance, she didn't trust it.

"It occurred to me after our little mishap yesterday that perhaps I might have come off too strong."

"You mean you behaved like an ass." She deliberately insulted him, more to regain her sense of equilibrium than anything.

"I admit some of my words might have been ill chosen. I apologize for that."

He did what? She could feel her eyes widen at his unexpected apology. "Um, thanks. I guess I should probably say sorry for massacring your hair."

He couldn't quite hide his wince at the reminder, and it was then that she took note of the fedora he wore. It matched the dove gray of his tailored suit, but still… She bit her lip lest she snicker. While a nice looking hat, it just didn't suit him.

"About my hair. It occurs to me that I owe you a second chance. A real chance to cut my hair. Albeit, probably shorter than I initially intended, given our misunderstanding."

"Excuse me? Did I just hear you say you want me to cut it? Now I know you're screwing with me."

"No tricks. Once I calmed down yesterday, I had a chance to reflect on what happened. I never truly gave you a chance. I let chauvinism cloud my judgment. But in my defense, my only other haircuts by women were done by my mother and aunts, whose idea of a trim involved a bowl and kitchen scissors."

Kira's turn to wince. "Ouch."

"Indeed. Perhaps that might help you to understand my hesitation. I should also admit I later spoke to your uncle at the barber shop. Initially, I'd planned to return to see him to have the damage blended. However, he assures me you are the best they have after Dominic."

She couldn't help but swell with pride at the praise. "I'm in pretty high demand." Or had been until her old shop got burned down under suspicious circumstances.

"What do you say we start over? Hi, my name is Arik." He stuck his hand out, and she stared at it.

Was he screwing with her? She shot him a wary glance but saw nothing in his face but sincerity, or a really good fake of it.

Given he was one of her granddad's clients, and only a bitch would throw his apology in his face, especially after what she'd done, she slipped her fingers into his massive grip.

An electrical tingle of awareness slid through her. Whatever his faults, she certainly couldn't deny her attraction to him.

"I'm Kira."

"Kira." The way he rolled the syllables of her name sent a tingle through her. Good thing he didn't host late night radio. There'd be a lot of tired women in the morning. "Well, Kira, now that we've been properly introduced, would you cut my hair? *Please.*"

Oh dear god, the way he said it. She almost leaned against the door for support. Her attraction to him was truly insane. But it wasn't his fault. She obviously had a problem.

I wonder if there's a pill I can take to prevent attraction to the wrong kind of guys.

"I don't think that's a good idea."

"But I need you to do it." Purred softly. He inched closer, and all her attention was taken by him, the towering height and breadth of him, a big man just the way she liked. His eyes were focused on her, intent, not afraid to meet her gaze, which was ridiculously sexy.

She wanted to press herself against him and soften the hard line of his lips, taste the teasing smile lurking at its corners.

How could she hope to cut his hair when all she wanted to do was run her hands over him?

She needed chaperones to keep her in line. "If you come back in about an hour when we open, I'll get you all fixed up."

"An hour? I don't suppose you could fit me in earlier somehow. I've got a business meeting this morning, and I'd really rather not go looking like this."

Amber eyes begged her. She hesitated. Those

eyes were way too seductive. She wished she could look away. Not give in.

But…

Technically, she could cut his hair now. She had the key to the shop. The only problem was no one else had arrived yet.

Did she dare let him in and cut his hair, alone? In other words, did she trust herself with him?

Am I seriously being such a coward? She really needed to take back some control over her hormones. She wasn't some giddy teenager who fawned over a boy. She was a woman, who knew how to handle herself with the opposite sex. She was also very well acquainted with the word 'no'.

She could resist his charm, and besides, it wouldn't be as if she would be alone with the big guy for long. Her uncle would meander in shortly, not to mention there were wide plate glass windows and people passing on the sidewalk.

Witnesses in case her hands thought to betray her again.

But what of her safety? Perhaps the flirting was a ruse. Perhaps his whole apology was to get her to lay down her guard.

While they spoke, the sidewalks had begun to fill up as people started their day.

If the big guy meant her ill, there would be witnesses.

However, glancing at his expression, which bore smoldering interest but none of the fury she recalled, she didn't get the impression he wanted to hurt her. At least not in painful ways. On the contrary, the hand that held hers, which he hadn't yet relinquished, stroked a thumb over her skin.

Do it.

Don't do it.

Her mind was split, but there was really only one choice. Kira wasn't one to usually pussy out. The man had swallowed his pride and apologized. The least she could do was help him out.

"Come in and I'll see what I can do." And by that, she meant do his hair, not do him.

Why did her spirits deflate at the thought?

He finally relinquished her hand, only to rub his thumb across her cheek. "Thank you. I appreciate this."

Ack. No, not the dimple. If she'd not caved before, she would have now as he unleashed the most devilish smile of thanks.

She forced herself to turn away. With shaking hands, she used the key and let them into the shop.

As she bustled around flicking on the lights, turning the sign to open, and pulling her hair items from the sanitized bag they were placed in by the cleaners, she tried to ignore him.

Not easy. He just seemed to consume the space of the room. No matter where he moved, she was intensely aware of him.

He hung up his outer jacket, revealing even more of his upper body. The dress shirt, made of a silk she could never hope to afford, molded to his chest and thickly muscled arms. He loosened his tie as he moved with a slow swagger to the barber chair.

He seated himself without prompting and proceeded to watch her in the mirror.

I should have made him wait. Too late now. She'd have to cut his hair.

A smile lurked at the corner of his lips as she fumbled the protective vinyl cape around him.

"I make you nervous," he stated.

Yes! "No. If you're talking about the clumsy hands, I'm still waiting for my caffeine to kick in," she lied.

For distraction, she plucked the hat from his head and winced as the shorn spot glared at her. She threaded her fingers through his silky locks, trying to see a way she could camouflage whilst keeping his preferred style. Alas, she'd trimmed a little too much. A part of her dreaded giving him the only option he had to fix it. She doubted he'd like her answer. "If I'm going to blend it, then we're going to have to cut it pretty much all off."

To his credit, he didn't erupt, although his face tightened, and she might have imagined a mournful meow, which made no sense since the shop didn't have a cat. Lazy, hairy things.

"Do what you must to my hair. I trust you."

The words shouldn't have sent a shiver—the erotic kind—down her spine, and yet they did, every word he uttered so sinfully sexy with his low baritone.

She resolved to cut only what she had to, and while he wouldn't sport a long, golden surfer mane by the time she was done, he'd look good. Better than good.

Way too delicious for words.

Seriously. As the hair flittered to the floor in a silky shower, his appearance changed. Grew more rugged. More masculine.

With every snip, she enhanced the craggy lines of his face, the strong squareness of his jaw, and the fact he had a perfectly shaped head.

When she was done, she took a step back and bit her lower lip as she surveyed the result.

My god he's attractive.

Or so she thought, but her opinion wasn't

really the one that mattered.

"What do you think?" she asked as she held the hand mirror at an angle behind him so as to give him a peek.

For a moment, he didn't say anything, just stared at his reflection in the mirror. "You know," he said slowly, "I've been sporting the same haircut for years. It was my look. My thing. So this is pretty drastic to me."

She could hear a 'but' coming, and she braced herself.

"But I think I wish I'd met you years ago. This is a really good haircut." He sounded surprised.

The tension in her frame eased. "So you like it?" She couldn't help but ask as she unsnapped the protective cover and removed it from him.

"Very much so. How much do I owe you?"

She lifted her hands and fluttered them. "Nothing. This one's on me."

He rose from the chair and towered over her. How petite he made her feel. "Nonsense. I insist."

"Consider it my apology for what happened." She would have taken a step away from his virile presence. However, the vanity with its rack of power hair tools blocked her path.

"You have to let me give you *something*."

The husky lowering of his voice sent a shiver through her.

"Refer your friends to the shop." She busied her hands with her tools, wiping them down and placing them on her tray.

He grabbed her hand and brought it to his mouth, placing a soft kiss on the top of it. "I already do refer this shop and have for years." He hummed the words against her skin.

She yanked her hand away. "Um, you know what, I should go and do something. Like fold towels." Or change her panties. Or...

She blinked as he said, "You and me. Dinner. Six p.m. I'll return to pick you up."

Before she could refuse, he left, broad shoulders barely fitting through the shop door. She could only stare at him as he hit the sidewalk. He paused and shot a glance at her through the window. He shot her his deadly dimple and winked.

She might have stood there staring dumbly for a while if her uncle hadn't come in and startled her. He'd used the alley entrance to access the hair shop.

"Kira, you're here early."

She whirled to face him, hoping nothing strange showed in her expression. "Yup, I'm here early because I need to leave early. Can you take my five o'clock?" Because she needed to be gone from here before Arik arrived and she did something foolish, like hope he kissed another part of her body. Forget her hands, he should embrace another part, a more appreciate part, like her lips.

Chapter Five

A sharp whistle stole Arik's attention from his task.

"Look who's a pretty boy again." Hayder strode into his office and immediately honed in on the new look.

A vain creature, not something he ever denied, Arik couldn't help but preen and show off. "Like it? I think it makes me look rather distinguished."

"And a total chick magnet too, dude. The girls on the telecom floor are all talking about it. Maybe I should think about getting a trim. Who did it?"

"A certain scissor-happy woman."

"No way. Don't tell me you stuck to your plan and confronted the broad who scalped you?"

"I did. Turns out she's quite talented when I'm not pissing her off."

Hayder whistled. "I'll say. I wouldn't mind letting her put her hands on me."

Arik clamped his lips before a growl could escape. What was wrong with his lion? "She's pretty busy."

"So? I'm making an appointment. What's the girl's name?" Hayder asked.

"Mine." Who'd said that? Surely not him. Arik almost looked around to see who else was in his office, but judging by Hayder's dropped jaw, there was only one culprit. His damned cat, who seemed to harbor a thing for the human girl.

Okay, maybe he should share the blame

because his lion wasn't the only one intrigued by Kira. While he'd initially gone to the hair shop this morning and lain in wait for a certain mouse as part of his revenge plot, he'd since had a change of mind. A drastic change of mind.

The haircut helped. She'd taken what he'd pissed and moaned about as a disaster of epic portions and turned it into a positive. If only he'd given her a chance yesterday before stomping home and ranting to anyone who would listen.

In retrospect, he might have overreacted. He could even almost feel guilty that he'd spent an evening alternating between roaring at his female family members who offered to tear Kira into chunks, to snarling at cousins, who almost peed on the carpet they were laughing so hard.

But the fantastic haircut wasn't the only reason for his change of mood. The sizzle of attraction between them, abetted by the scent of her arousal, which she couldn't hope to hide from a predator, had evaporated his initial ire into…

He wasn't sure what he felt, other than a need to see more of Kira.

Yes. More Kira. Naked. With lots of licking involved.

"Mine? That's an odd name?" Hayder mused aloud. "I don't think I've ever come across it. Is it foreign?"

"Don't be an idiot. Her name is Kira, but I don't want you going near her." Because Hayder was a ladies man, and he'd hate to have to kill his beta. But he would if he had to.

No touch. Mine.

Oops, he might have growled that part aloud.

Hayder laughed. "Holy smokes, dude. What the hell happened this morning? Yesterday you were all 'vengeance is mine,' and today it's all 'she is mine'."

Arik resorted to a white lie. "I can't have my proper revenge if you're meddling. So stay away from her. I'll let you know when I'm done."

Which will be never.

He really needed to have a talk with his feline side. It was getting territorial about the girl, which wasn't an option.

As alpha of his pride, when Arik did settle down, it would be for political reasons and with someone carrying the felidaethropy gene. In other words, another lion, or at least a feline shifter, like him. It was what shapeshifters did to keep the bloodlines pure.

It wasn't that humans and shifters couldn't marry and have babies. They could, and did, but there was a catch. Only about ten percent of these mixed matings would bear offspring with the animal gene. Given their low population numbers, they couldn't afford their strongest to hook up with humans.

Even if they were tempting, and cute.

However, with all that said, it didn't mean he couldn't play with Kira. Cats did so enjoy teasing and toying with mice. *Grab her sweet tail and make her squeak.*

Thing was, no matter how many times he reminded himself of the impossibility of them having a relationship, he spent the day thinking about her. And the more he thought about her, the more it occurred to him that the feisty woman he'd met wouldn't necessarily behave like others.

Arik was used to having females throw themselves at him. If it wasn't his wealth that attracted them, then it was his power, and, no, it wasn't vain to admit that he wasn't hard to look at.

When it came to the opposite sex, Arik didn't

lack for attention. However, even he had to admit Kira wasn't like the women he usually dated. For one, she tried to stand him up.

Parked in a chair in a café, with a clear view of the barbershop, he saw her exit just before five, furtively peeking in both directions.

Was his mouse hoping to escape him?

Not this time. Throwing some bills on the table, Arik left the café and shadowed Kira, instinct having him duck behind bus shelters or inside shop doors just before she craned to peek over her shoulder.

Being a human didn't mean her instincts didn't try to warn her she was being stalked. However, she couldn't tell for sure because she was dealing with the king of predators. Arik knew how to blend in and track his prey. He also knew when to pounce, which was when she least expected it.

"Running somewhere?"

She squeaked and stumbled but didn't fall, as he shot out a hand to grab her.

She whirled to face him. "What the hell are you doing?"

"I could ask the same of you. I thought the plan was to meet at the shop. Yet here you are picking up fish? Got a date with a cat?" He loved the irony of his words but hated her reply.

"I'm actually more of a dog lover."

"Cats are nicer."

"They're snotty creatures who think they own you."

How well she already knew his breed.

"And they're always hacking up hairballs. No thank you. I'll take an obedient dog any day."

Obedience was overrated, unless it was from

his underlings. Arik preferred to be the one giving the commands. She'd soon learn that. "Am I to assume you were planning to get changed and return before six for our dinner date?"

Judging by the expression on her face? No.

"Listen, Arik. You're a nice guy and all, and I'm glad we worked things out, but I really don't think we should be going to dinner."

"How remiss of me. Of course not."

"So you understand."

"Perfectly. After a long day of work, you're probably tired and want to just relax in something comfortable on your couch."

"Exactly." She appeared so relieved, which was what made his next words so enjoyable.

"Fabulous idea. We'll order in instead." He used the tip of a finger to lift her hanging jaw. "Any preference? Chinese? Indian? Italian?"

"I think you misunderstand."

He leaned in, totally and intentionally invading her space, close enough to hear the rapid flutter of her pulse and to see her eyes dilate as she stared at him. As for her scent? He could have drooled as anxiety, and anticipation, heightened the aroma of her musky arousal. "I understand that you are trying to avoid me. Problem is, I won't let that happen. We are going to eat together. The question is, will we do it in the privacy of your apartment, just the two of us, alone with a bed nearby? Or will you be a frightened mouse and insist on somewhere public?"

She sucked in a breath. "I am not scared of you."

"So we're dining in?"

"No. If I have to eat with you, then we're going to a restaurant."

"Very well. Name one."

He should have known by the smirk that crossed her lips that she would get him back for his ambush, and she did.

"LongHorn."

His steak house competition.

Chapter Six

Exactly how did Kira end up sitting across from Arik in a booth with a menu in hand?

This was the exact opposite of what should have happened. She'd had it all planned. She'd leave early. Her uncle would tell Arik, if he showed up, that she was sick. The big guy would forget about her, and she'd go on with her new life.

Except, he'd suspected she'd do something devious and lain in wait for her.

She didn't know whether to be flattered or call the cops. She also couldn't help but be impressed he'd gauged her so well. Many of the guys she'd dated, or who'd shown an interest over the years, never truly got to understand her. They assumed she was just like all the other girls.

Wrong. Kira was special. And not in the 'she needed medication to stop hearing the voices' kind of way. She was unique, she did things her own way—even if sometimes her own way meant taking a coward's way out. Then again, Gregory had taught her well. Which led her mind back to thinking about Arik.

Persistent big guy who was alluring, like a chocolate-dipped cone. She just wanted to nibble and lick.

Ardent interest was all well and good, but what if he turned out to be another psycho just like her ex?

The fact that she'd gotten Arik to agree to take

her to a competing restaurant spoke volumes. Despite his evident dislike at the way she'd maneuvered him, he'd taken it with good grace.

And now would make her pay. Such a devious and handsome devil.

He asked for and received a booth in the farthest corner where the lighting was dim, a romantic ambiance for lovers.

But we're not lovers.

Yet. Because, truthfully, the man seriously attracted her.

She could have slapped herself. No. *Bad Kira.* She wasn't at a point in her life where she needed any kind of commitment.

Getting a little ahead of yourself, are we? The chiding of her own inner voice reined her in. After all, he'd flirted, but who said he was looking for a relationship? It could be he just wanted a little naked companionship. Although why he'd choose her, she couldn't fathom.

Kira had no illusions when it came to her image. She was cute, on that she would agree. However, she was about thirty pounds too heavy to be considered perfectly shaped, and her hips were a touch wide when considered against her bust. She had birthing hips, or so her one aunt said.

That wasn't exactly something Kira considered a compliment or a positive attribute for her dating resume. She did have nice hair, though, and pretty eyes. "A nice-looking girl," as her uncle liked to say. Which, translated, meant she wasn't the type of woman that guys, especially billionaire tycoon types like Arik, chased after.

Unless he liked the challenge.

Could perhaps her refusal to give him the time

of day be that which drew him?

"You look way too serious for someone trying to choose an appetizer," he murmured.

The soft purr of his voice should come with a warning label much like they showed on TV. *Please note that the hunk sitting across from you may cause heart palpitations, clammy hands, wet panties, and a hunger for things not meant to be eaten in public.*

She steeled herself before she peeked up and caught his gaze over the edge of her menu. "Just debating on whether I want a salad to start or some stuffed mushrooms."

"Or you could just nibble on me," he said with a wink.

"Arik!" His bold words shocked and did nothing to stem the arousal she already fought. Heat flushed her, and she could only imagine the color of her cheeks. It wasn't hard to feign embarrassment and bury her face in the menu again.

"Oh, come now, mouse. Don't act so outraged."

"You just propositioned me."

"No, I was just being honest about what we're both thinking."

He guessed. No way could he know she desired him. "I don't know what you're talking about."

He made a noise. "I don't know why you feel a need to pretend."

"Pretend what?"

"That we're not attracted to each other."

"I don't know where you got that idea. You're an interesting guy, sure, but that's it."

"Liar." And he proved it by grabbing her hand and stroking his thumb over the skin. She couldn't hide a tremble at the contact. "I touch you, and you shiver."

She really needed to shave that expressive and sexy eyebrow of his. Maybe then she wouldn't get an urge to fan herself.

"Could be repugnance."

He let out a short laugh. "You and I both know that's not true."

Since denial wasn't getting her anywhere, she changed her tactics. "Fine. So you're attractive. I still don't think we should take things any further. We are obviously from two different worlds."

"Yes." He didn't even try to deny it.

What a letdown. She'd expected more argument. *Which says what about me exactly?* "So why do this? Why are you so determined to wine, dine, and screw me?" She deliberately made it sound crude, anything to break the spell between them.

"Screw? I have more finesse than that, I assure you, mouse. When we do come together, I promise it will be an event of sensual delight."

"Let's say I let that happen. That we have sex, then what? I've already told you I don't want to date. I can't." Not until she could be sure the mistakes of her past wouldn't return to bug her.

"Can't?" It figured he'd hone in on the one word. "Are you seeing someone?" Funny how he bit the query out, as if angry, and his eyes flashed amber in the dim light.

Almost catlike. Totally crazy. It was probably some weird trick of the light, just like people sometimes got red devil eyes in pictures.

"No, I'm not seeing someone. Not anymore. But let's just say my last relationship terminated in a rather ugly fashion." Understatement of the century.

"Given what he put me through, I need a break from the whole dating thing."

"Then we won't date. I, too, am not at a point in my life where I'm looking for a forever after. However, I wouldn't mind a companion for passionate get-togethers."

It took her a moment, and she might have blinked a few times before she said, "Are you asking me to be your fuck buddy?

He made a moue of distaste. "I think the correct term is my mistress."

Kira couldn't help it. She giggled.

"What's so funny?" he asked, a frown drawing his brows together.

"This whole conversation. You do realize this is totally abnormal, right?"

"On the contrary, I think it is refreshing in this day and age that a man and woman who find themselves attracted to each other can have a civilized discussion about engaging in a sexual partnership that doesn't involve any emotional attachments or long-term commitments."

Said with utter seriousness. A mistress. Negligee wearing, sultry-voiced hussy who greets her tailored-suit lover. Passionate wild times, followed by jewelry and a quick escape by him.

The mental image proved too much. She laughed harder.

And, apparently, he didn't like it.

"Stop laughing," he ordered, his stern voice just as sexy as his flirty one.

"Is this where I start calling you sir? Or master?" She chortled and, to her mortification, snorted, which in turn led to even more mirth.

Practically weeping she was laughing so hard,

she didn't immediately note his action until he slid onto the booth seat beside her. She turned to glance at him, and he took advantage, cupping her chin in his hand. He silenced her with a kiss.

Suddenly nothing was funny, but everything was on fire.

The hand gripping her chin slid until it cupped the side of her face, cradling her in the palm of his large hand. Her lips parted at the insistent coaxing of his. Apparently he wanted a taste because his tongue trailed the length of her lips, tracing them, before dipping to dance with hers.

She kept her hands clasped in her lap, fingers digging in tightly. She feared letting them loose. Knew they would hone in on his body and stroke the hard planes she could glimpse under his dress shirt. Make a mockery of her continued insistence they shouldn't get together.

He, however, had no such fear. While one hand stroked the skin of her cheek, the other palmed the space just below her ribcage. He'd wrapped his arm around her, her slightly plump frame no issue, not given where his hand rested, and inched upward.

The fabric separating them did nothing to impede the breath-catching anticipation of his hand reaching to cup an aching breast. His mouth sucked her little sound of pleasure. She squirmed on her seat, thighs pressed tight together. But it did nothing to relieve the building, aching pressure between her legs.

But do you know what did act as a bucket of cold water?

Getting caught.

Chapter Seven

Roar. He stifled the sound but only barely. Arik could have easily and happily killed the waiter who cleared his throat and interrupted his kiss with Kira.

"Are you ready to order?"

Ready to order a can of whoop ass. Breaking the lip lock, Arik glared at the young man who stood at their tableside, pad of paper in hand.

Beside him, Kira panted softly, looking much too lovely with her flushed cheeks, bright eyes, and swollen lips. She recovered more quickly than he liked.

"I'd like a martini please. A big one. I'll start with a Caesar salad, extra garlic. Loaded baked potato, and twelve ounce porterhouse, rare." As she ordered, studiously ignoring him, Arik leaned back against the leatherette seat. He draped an arm over her shoulder, a possessive gesture that went against his speech to Kira earlier.

Yes, he might have stated he didn't want anything permanent. He didn't need the headache a steady relationship would bring—like expectations of him showing up on time or buying gifts. Sometimes a man just wanted something easy and uncomplicated. Sometimes he just wanted sex. In this case, he really wanted Kira as a lover. Problem was, a part of him, a slim part, possibility wanted her more than just naked in his bed.

Keep her.

Totally crazy and against everything he knew, everything he was taught. Arik knew what his pride would ask him to do, the women at least. They'd tell him to end it. Now. Just get up and walk away. Reinforce her belief he was an arrogant jerk.

He was, and with any other woman, he might have done it. But this was Kira. And, for some reason, Kira was different. The various layers to her intrigued him.

Must find out her secrets. Must find a way to chisel through her shields, which were fully engaged at the moment as she sat there, prim and innocent with her hands laced in her lap. A concentrated attempt to pretend as if the kiss hadn't happened.

He let his fingers tickle her nape, and she shivered, unable to hide her reaction to him.

"And you, sir, what will you have?"

Was that idiot still there, ruining his pleasant thoughts? "I'll have what she's having, times two."

Magic words that saw the waiter finally leaving. "Where were we?" He purred the words, something his lion form just couldn't do. However, make no mistake, this wasn't the contented purr of a housecat getting a treat. This was the purr of a predator buttering up his conquest.

Buttered her so well, she slipped away and feigned indifference.

"So what do you think of the décor?"

Wood. Lots of it, and he didn't mean just the walls. "I think you're avoiding what just happened. I think we should discuss it."

"Discuss what? It wasn't a big deal. You kissed me."

"It was more than a kiss."

"If you say so." As she replied, she continued

to studiously ignore him.

So stubborn. He went silent and stared at her, knowing it wouldn't take long to drive her nuts.

She lasted longer than expected, but finally, she snapped. "What do you want from me?"

"I thought I made that clear. You. Me. Somewhere private."

Tilting her head, she glanced his way. Her lips pursed. "You're very stubborn."

"I know. Are we continuing the alphabet of my attributes, such as handsome, impressive, jocular."

"You're not that funny."

"Says the woman who was snorting a moment ago."

"Conceited."

"That doesn't start with a K."

"No, but kookoo does."

"We made it to L. Lover."

He grinned as she rolled her eyes. "Good grief. You won't stop trying to seduce me until you get what you want, will you?"

"No." Firmly stated.

She heaved a heavy sigh. "Fine."

"What do you mean, fine?"

"We'll eat dinner and then have sex. But don't take too long would you with the humping and grunting. I've got to work in the morning, and I'll need a shower."

That didn't sound exactly seductive. He frowned. "You make it sound like a chore."

She angled her head sideways so she could smirk at him. "I guess that depends on who's doing all the work. In this case, that would be you. So you'd better make it good, or no amount of begging and big, pleading eyes will get you seconds."

Begging? Did she think he begged her? Fur ruffled, he slid back to his seat across from her so he could better read her expression.

She, of course, misunderstood his strategic move.

"Did I prick someone's ego?"

"We'll see who gets pricked," he muttered ominously.

She caught the innuendo. The blush brightening her cheeks brought some of his cockiness back.

She's not the only one who can verbally tease.

But she made eating a whole new form of torture.

Chapter Eight

He's going to pounce.

It sure seemed that way to Kira. She'd thought once the food arrived that the sexual tension between them would diminish. Sure, the thrown verbal challenges kept the lid on the simmering pot, but it wasn't enough to douse the fire.

The man plain fascinated her. He took her rebukes and teasing with mock anger, sometimes affront, oftentimes laughter. Then he retaliated in kind, not tossing false flattery her way but, instead, tossing out outrageous suggestions.

She had almost reached the point that she needed to fan her flushed skin when the food arrived. Lots of it. Arik had ordered double her meal, which wasn't small. They started with the salad. Not a sexy food, anyone would agree.

And yet, when she licked some of the creamy Caesar sauce from her bottom lip, she could have sworn Arik groaned. He definitely inserted a foot between her legs. He'd slipped off his shoe under the table, and his toes, more agile than she would have expected, wiggled their way up her leg. She caught it before it hit the apex of her thighs.

"What are you doing?"

"Who me? Nothing." A man of his bearing shouldn't have the ability to look innocent and devilish at the same time.

She tried to budge his foot. It didn't move. Actually, it wiggled higher. "Don't you dare."

"I was just looking for a warm spot. Their air conditioning is set a touch too cold for me."

"I am not a toe warmer."

"You're right. You're more than that. Personally, I'd much prefer to have you wrapped all over me."

And that was the way the small talk went during the salad. As for his foot, she kept it from pressing all the way, but only because he didn't insist. She, on the other hand, found herself hard-pressed to not slide on the bench and let his toes press against a certain aching part of her body.

The man took foreplay to a whole new level— while they were both still clothed!

However, she'd discovered his weakness. Licking her lips was one. How avidly he watched the swipe of her tongue. Yet it was her groan of enjoyment at her first bite of the perfectly seasoned, flame-kissed steak that had him making the oddest growling sound.

She finished chewing and swallowing the succulent hunk of meat before asking, "Are you all right? You seem to be a little tense."

"Nothing little about my tenseness, mouse."

"Men! Always so concerned with the size when it's all about the tongue." She could have crawled under the table when the words—loosened by a very delicious martini—spilled from her lips.

"No worries, mouse, when it comes to licking, I am a master."

To that, there was no reply—because she sure as hell wasn't going with the one that popped into her head of, 'Prove it.'

Their verbal foreplay during the main part of their meal was nothing compared to dessert. It seemed he'd tired of sitting alone. Once again, he crowded her, sharing her bench.

"You're in my space."

"I am. Get used to it. I like to cuddle."

His claim had her gaping. He took the moment to spoon a mouthful of dessert into her mouth. Caramel-topped cheesecake. Her favorite.

She groaned. Loudly. With great pleasure.

Something growled. Softly. And then he kissed her, to her pleasure.

It proved a short kiss. She protested, and another spoon of sweetness was fed to her. Followed immediately by another embrace. Sugar goodness. Hot kiss. Ooh, some tongue. Some groping.

A voice asking if he could get them anything else—the waiter seriously wanted to die.

As if sharing one mind, they both snapped, "The check."

Arik tossed bills on the table, much more than needed for their meal. His haste to get them out of there proved quite flattering. They made it out of the restaurant and around a corner before he pushed her against a wall. His hard lips claimed hers in a torrid kiss, which sucked all reason from her mind. His large hands cupped her bottom, pulling her against him, outlining the evidence of his arousal. His very large arousal.

She clung to him, fingers gripping the muscles of his broad shoulders. Forget her earlier determination to stay away. He was right about one thing; she wanted him. Wanted a night of passionate and wild sex.

A no-strings, pleasurable event just for the hell of it.

But she'd prefer it not be in public.

"I know of an empty bed," she whispered brazenly against his mouth.

"A bed would be nice, but I don't know if we'll make it," was his reply.

"What's that supposed to mean?"

"You'll see."

Why did his ominous words make her channel clench and quiver in pre-orgasmic delight?

Chapter Nine

There were times Arik thanked the fact he didn't always follow trends. Times like now.

Unlike many men of wealth, Arik didn't much care for tiny sports cars. For one, he was a big man who liked his space, and for another, he wanted something with substance protecting him when on the road, hence his purchase of a fully equipped Escalade, and he meant fully equipped. Buttery-soft leather seats, tinted windows, a kick-ass sound system, and his favorite part, which all felines coveted, heated seats.

He had another reason to thank his foresight in buying a big vehicle, given the very spacious interior and custom-crafted wide front seat that made it easy for him to haul Kira onto his lap.

"I thought we were going to my place," she protested.

"We will. In a minute." Or two. Or three. Right now, he had no interest in driving anywhere. All he wanted was to continue their kiss.

Lips clinging, hands stroking, they made out in the front seat of his truck and steamed the windows.

It was her choice to turn in his lap and straddle him. An excellent choice because it pressed her heated core against him. They both moaned at the contact. A few layers of clothes made the teasing rub only more arousing.

His hands slid under her sweater, and he felt her shiver as he stroked the smooth skin of her back. Of course, he had an ulterior motive in his roaming. It took but a second to unsnap the closure on her bra.

"What are you doing?" She recoiled from him, eyes at half-mast and her lips swollen from his kiss.

"What's it look like I'm doing? Getting to second base." Her breasts, freed for his touch, weighed nicely in his palms. The stroke of his thumbs over the peaks had her sucking in a breath.

How he wanted to lift her shirt and taste. Yet even he knew better than to denude her in public. Someone might see her, *and then I'd have to kill them.*

Mine. And this lion didn't want to share. Just like the man didn't want to stop.

A rational part of him said he should pause in his seduction for a few minutes and drive them somewhere with a bed, but need drove him at this point, not logic. A need to have this woman. Now.

A desire she shared.

She threw herself forward, hair flying in a dark arc, her hands grabbing his jaw on either side, drawing him close for a searing kiss.

How hotly she burned.

He couldn't help but let one hand leave the tempting swell of her breast and span the indent of her waist. How he loved her voluptuous hour-glass shape, so womanly and desirable. He wanted to explore every inch of her curves, with his fingers, his body, his lips...

For the moment, he had to content himself with what he could reach, given their position. He ran his fingers along the waistband of her yoga pants. Stretchy fabric, perfect for his hand to dip farther. He encountered a naughty panty line, a G-string by the feel of it. So mouse liked sexy underthings. Nice. Very nice. He'd have to remember to remove it with his teeth later. For now, he let his fingers quest under the scrap of lace, moving from the rounded swell of her buttocks around her hip. He wanted to feel her molten core against his fingertips, but their position was too awkward for him to cup her properly.

So he moved her. Manhandled her to suit his needs. He didn't ask or explain, just grabbed her and spun her on his lap until she faced away. She might have protested had he not immediately sent his hand questing down the front of her pants.

He cupped her mound, and she let out a soft sigh of pleasure.

Hot. How hot she burned against his hand, and wet, too, the cream of her arousal moistening his fingers. She enjoyed his touch. He could tell by the way she leaned back against him, head resting on his shoulder, her throat exposed, a long white expanse of temptation.

How he wanted to bite. Lions did so love a good nibble during sex, especially when they wanted to show a claim.

For a moment, rationality swam to the surface, overriding his desire, reminding him that Kira was human. Kira wasn't his mate. Kira was squirming against his hand, which, in turn, meant her luscious, round bottom squirmed against him.

Rational thought sank as need overpowered and drowned it.

Just a little taste. He pressed his lips against the tender column of her throat and sucked at the skin as his fingers pressed against her sex. She let out a small cry, and he felt the reaction in her sex. Moist heat honeyed his digits, rendering them slick, perfect for sliding against her swollen pleasure button.

Her breathing became even shorter, more ragged. She made small noises as she squirmed. He anchored her in place, the torture of her rubbing against his erection from her spot on his lap not as bad as the torture from feeling her cream on his fingers but unable to take a lick.

Since Arik couldn't bury his tongue into her sex, he contented himself by penetrating her with his finger. He inserted one. Two. The walls of her channel clung tight to him, and his shaft grew even harder in reaction. How he longed to bury himself in her welcoming sex. How he wanted to feel the walls of her channel fisting his cock.

For once, he didn't let his selfish desires rule him. In this instance, her pleasure came first. He intended to bring her to climax, and enjoy every moment of it.

As he sucked on the soft skin of her neck, he pumped his fingers in and out. A slow, steady penetration. He savored the tenseness invading her limbs. He groaned at the suction of her sex.

He almost roared when her orgasm hit, the ripple of her pleasure squeezing his fingers and coating them in erotic cream. He barely held back from nipping her neck, instead humming his appreciation against her skin.

As her shudders subsided, and his cock throbbed, anxious for its turn, he withdrew his fingers from her quivering sex and brought them to his mouth for a lick.

Delicious.

And to think, that was just an appetizer to the main course.

He couldn't wait for round two, in a bed.

He placed a dazed Kira in the passenger seat and buckled her in. Pride suffused him at her sated expression. Desire pulsed through him as he imagined what would happen next.

Impatient, he started his truck and tore out of the parking lot, tires squealing in his haste. The quicker he moved, the faster he'd get her naked and have her making sweet, pleasurable sounds again and ease away the crease forming on her brow.

Alas, fate conspired against him. The bitch. She was probably in cahoots with the female members of his pride.

Chapter Ten

Coming back down to reality sucked. While short, the drive was still long enough for Kira to question what the heck she'd done and was planning to do.

She'd let a guy she barely knew bring her to orgasm in his truck in a parking lot. In plain view! *What is wrong with me?*

And why wasn't she more appalled by her actions?

That had to be the worst part. She didn't harbor an ounce of shame at all, even though she'd acted like a hussy. Despite her turmoil over her actions, when he asked for her address, she gave it. No hesitation, nor did she pull away when he grabbed her left hand and placed it on his muscled thigh. He anchored it there by placing his heavier hand atop it. The intimate contact thrilled her.

Despite her recent climax, her desire for him remained unquenched. Who cared if she barely knew him and he wanted nothing more than hot, pleasurable sex? He offered exactly what she wanted. A good time with no strings or expectations. Given recent events, she could use an evening of mindless fun.

At least she wanted it until he pulled to a stop in front of her uncle's shop. It took only a glance outside her window to change her mind.

It wasn't the large plate glass window with its blue-lettered Fresh From The Brine sign that caught her attention, or the front door of the store with its posted hours and 'Closed' placard. Instead, her gaze zeroed in on the unassuming little door alongside that she used after hours to get to her place. Personally, she preferred the inside access because the outside stairs were ridiculously steep. But when the shop was closed, she had to resort to the other entrance to her place.

Yet, it wasn't dread of that huffing and puffing flight of stairs that had her desire shutting off abruptly. It was the sight of smeared letters, running in red rivulets, on the white portal and inset glass pane that made her heart drop.

Bitch slut. Only one person ever called her that.

How could *he* have found her? She'd fled across the country. Taken on an apartment without a lease. Nothing was in her name. And yet, that message, that level of hate… She knew of only one person who'd do this.

The knowledge that Gregory might lurk killed any thoughts of spending a pleasant evening with the man by her side. She couldn't draw Arik into the messy thing known as her life. But what excuse could she use to foist Arik off? Somehow saying, "You need to leave because my psycho ex-boyfriend might be stalking me," didn't seem like a great way to end an evening that should have finished in her bed with a lot less clothing.

Not to mention, being a guy, Arik would probably go all macho on her and insist on protecting her. Men did so love to beat on their chests to proclaim their superiority to others, which might prove sexy—especially if shirtless—but was not what she needed right now.

So how to douse the sizzle he still felt, and escape? She knew only one sure-fire way to dampen his libido. The ultimate cock blocker: good ol' Mom. "Shoot, you can't come up tonight. I'm afraid I just remembered I've got to call my mother. She's having some big premenopausal issues, you know hot flashes and stuff. I kind of promised we'd chat later tonight. Completely forgot. Real sorry. We'll have to get together another time," she blurted out in a rapid stream of words as she let herself out of Arik's truck.

Before she could stand before the door to cover the graffiti, she felt a presence at her back. Automatic fear had her squeak until she realized it was simply Arik, who'd moved more rapidly than expected. Somehow he'd exited his vehicle without her hearing and stood looming over her. Knowing it was him did nothing to quell her rapidly beating heart.

"I told you before not to lie to me."

She whirled and tried to stand in front of the evidence and reason for her lie. "Okay, so maybe my mother's not expecting a call. I just didn't want to hurt your feelings by saying I changed my mind. Woman's prerogative you know." It sounded weak even to her and didn't budge him one inch.

Amber eyes fixed her. "Move."

"What for?"

"So I can see what you're hiding."

"Me? Hiding something?" She tried an innocent bat of her lashes.

It didn't work. With a hand placed on either side of her waist, he hefted her and put her out of the way, revealing the dripping message in all its profane glory.

"What the heck is that?" He stabbed a finger at the door.

"Teenagers bringing down property values," she said, followed by a feeble attempt at a laugh.

He didn't buy it, judging by his frown. "This isn't a random message. It's aimed at you, and it's got you scared."

"No, I'm not." She should have known better than to fib. Her mother always did say she sucked at it.

Arik didn't buy it for a second. "I'm not an idiot. You're scared because you know who left this."

"Maybe," she hedged. He crossed his arms and stared her down. It was impressive as stares went. She shrugged. "Okay, so I have an inkling. But it should be impossible. He's supposed to be out west. There's no way he could know where I am."

"'He' being the ex-boyfriend that didn't end well?"

She shrugged. "It's possible, or this really could just be a random act of neighborhood art."

"Art is actual images or initials, not the words bitch slut smeared in blood."

She winced as he said it aloud. But then his words penetrated. Blood? Surely not. She bit her lower lip in worry. "We don't know that it's blood. It could be ketchup."

"I work with meat. I know blood when I see it. Has this guy threatened you before?"

How much to tell him? Already, Arik seemed awfully mad. Not at her, though. Someone was pumped up on testosterone, a true male reacting to a perceived threat. Cute, but did she really need another man in her life causing chaos? Even if Arik offered her protection, she wasn't sure she wanted his help.

Having him around, possibly where Gregory could see him, would just cause more trouble.

Gregory had deep jealousy issues. Real deep. Only one of the many reasons why she'd dumped him. Problem was, Gregory didn't take the rejection well.

"It's nothing you have to worry about. It's my problem, and I'll deal with it. I'll contact the local cops and see if his restraining order only applies for my old place of residence. If I can't have it transferred, then I'll just get a new one. Problem solved."

A muscle ticked on the side of his jaw. "Not problem solved. This guy's obviously a nut job if he's followed you across the continent just to threaten you."

"Well, I wouldn't exactly call this a threat, more like a judgment on my character."

Was that a growl she heard?

"Kira, why are you deliberately downplaying this?"

"Because this isn't your problem. It's mine, okay? And one I should have apparently dealt with instead of running away. Stupid me, I thought if I left, the whole out-of-sight, out-of-mind thing would work. That Gregory would leave me alone. I was wrong. So now I'll deal with it. Alone."

His lips tightened. "Not alone."

"Yes, alone. This has nothing to do with you. We're not a couple, remember? Which means you have no say in my personal life, and this is personal. So now, if you'll excuse me, I'm going to go upstairs, call the cops, and deal with this. By myself."

With that, she unlocked her door and let herself into the tiny vestibule. She whirled to slam the door shut behind her, making sure to lock it while ignoring Arik's stare through the blood-marked glass. And, yes, he stared. Silently, but still his eyes drilled a message that she felt between her shoulder blades as she trudged up the stairs, one that said, *You're being stubborn.*

Yup. But she couldn't help herself. Blame her mother who'd raised her that way.

When she got to the top of the stairs, huffing and puffing, the steepness still not any easier than the first time she'd tackled them, she could admit to herself a hiccup of fear as the closed door to her apartment taunted her. What lay beyond it? Safety, or did she walk into danger?

Maybe I should have had Arik come up with me, just to check.

I'm a big girl. I can handle this. She, and the can of mace she pulled from her purse. She held it in a ready-to-spray position as she let herself into her apartment.

Nobody jumped out at her, which meant she didn't have to change her panties. Kegels tightly clenched, she immediately flicked a light switch and illuminated the tiny entrance. Still nobody, but there were too many shadows for her liking, dark corners where anything, or anyone, could hide.

Practically hyperventilating, she turned on every single lamp she had, even the bathroom vanity lights. Nobody lurked in the corners, nobody popped out of her closet or flung back the shower curtain brandishing a knife to the music from *Psycho*.

The undisturbed apartment should have proven reassuring, yet the fear wouldn't vanish.

He knows where I am. He hasn't given up.

What would Gregory do next?

Unlike what she'd told Arik, she didn't bother calling the cops. She already knew what they'd say. Until Gregory did something, they couldn't act. The message on her door wouldn't count. She couldn't prove he'd left the bloody message, just like she couldn't prove all the other things he'd done back home—the dead flowers on her front step, the slashed tires on her car. When it came to stalking— and inspiring terror—Gregory played the game all too well.

Alone, with no one to watch, or judge, Kira finally gave in to trembling fear. It took over her limbs, turning muscles into quivering jelly, and sent her slumping to the floor. But she didn't note the hardness under her buttocks or the coldness of the plaster as she leaned against the wall—a wall that would prevent a sneak attack from behind. She drew her knees to her chest and hugged them, rocking slowly as tears streamed down her cheeks. Relief and terror all rolled into one.

She might have played the part of strong, capable woman to Arik, but the truth was Kira was terrified.

In moving hundreds of miles, she'd truly hoped to have left her past behind. For a moment that evening, with Arik teasing and delighting all her senses, she'd almost let herself think about giving Arik a little more than just her body. Maybe she could think of starting over.

Wrong. She couldn't move on with her life. Not now. Not with Arik. Not with anyone. Heck, if it weren't for the fact she'd need her paycheck from the barbershop, she'd be packing a bag and fleeing tonight.

Gregory wasn't working with a full deck, not

where she was concerned. He'd already proven that when he burned down her hair shop back home. Kira didn't care what the fire marshal claimed. *Rats chewing on the wiring my ass.*

Would her ex-boyfriend resort to the same trick twice? She couldn't bear it if her granddad lost the shop he'd worked in for forty years because of her. But with Gregory, anything was possible.

What's his plan? What does he want?

He knew she didn't want him, so why wouldn't he leave her alone? What would he do next? He'd left a message, but she doubted he was done. The question was, would he let her stew in fear before making his next move, or was he already implementing the next step in his plot for revenge?

I'm an idiot for staying here. She should have gone to a hotel for the night. Too late now. She didn't dare leave the relative safety of her apartment.

Fear kept her awake for a while. She watched the window that had access to the fire escape, but the bright lights in her apartment didn't let her see much but a reflection of her apartment. For all she knew, he was crouched out there, watching. Waiting for her to fall asleep. To be vulnerable.

She flinched at every sound the old building made as it creaked through the night. Fatigue tried to claim her. She nodded off in spurts, only to startle awake, certain he'd come for her.

Morning couldn't come soon enough. And then she had some decisions to make.

Chapter Eleven

Protect.

That was Arik's second instinct after he managed to control his first one, which roared *Kill!*

Satisfying, but also against human laws. Spoilsports.

Still, something needed to be done. It didn't take a finely honed sense of smell to perceive the terror emanating from Kira. A simple act of graffiti shouldn't have been enough to terrorize his fearless mouse. But when she'd divulged the possibility the threat was left by an ex-suitor, he started to form a picture.

A picture that required more information. But he couldn't exactly demand it from her, which was the only reason why he let her flee to her apartment alone. It went against his better judgment, but he allowed it, having to content himself with the knowledge he wasn't far.

Logic, however, didn't soothe his inner savage beast. The scent of blood, and not just blood, but the blood of a wolf, drove him to the brink. Whoever had left the message was a Lycan. An enemy. One who'd not just dared to threaten *his* woman, but dared to come into his territory.

While Arik might not rule this city's wolf pack, the canine group, few in number because not many took to city life, knew better than to cross him.

Rules stated all Lycans coming into his city had to report in to the pack leader. The leader, in turn, then notified Arik, who, being a gracious feline king, allowed the visitor to stay, so long as he or she behaved. But cross the line and…

Let's just say Arik enforced his laws, which had been created to protect them all from discovery. The fact that someone dared to show up to cause mischief didn't sit well at all. Especially since it meant Kira was dealing with more than just an ordinary ex-boyfriend who refused to let go.

Another tries to claim her. But would fail. He'd make sure of that.

Arik had to ignore his lion, which chuffed and chafed, demanding they follow her and stay close to her side. An instinct honed over the years said she was safe in her apartment. The lock showed no signs of tampering, and a quick check of the alleyway didn't reveal any recent scent of anyone trying to climb the fire escape. The wolf had left his message and left.

But where Kira was concerned, assumptions weren't enough. He needed to be sure. To see her safe for himself.

For that end, he clambered up the rickety metal structure the fire code demanded, staying out of sight of the well-lit window on the second floor. A quick peek inside showed a small, plainly furnished place. He noted no signs of violence and heard nothing but soft, gut-wrenching sobs.

She cries. A silent roar of frustration.

How he fought hard not to barrel into Kira's place and sweep her into his arms, promise her she had nothing to fear. However, she'd made it clear she wanted to be alone, and breaking in now would do nothing to ease her trepidation. And given she clutched a can of pepper mace, any attempt to get at her might prove unpleasant for them both.

Instead, he would be her hidden protector, standing guard from outside. *Don't fear, mouse. I'll watch over you. You won't come to harm.* He couldn't promise the same for the guy scaring her.

A guy who needed a full name and a face. Arik made some phone calls, and no, he didn't care that it was late and people might be abed.

If they worked for him, then they were fair game.

"Hayder." He didn't bother with niceties when his second answered. "I need you to find out what you can about Kira…" He paused as he realized he didn't even know her last name. Dammit.

"Kira who?"

"I don't know her last name, but it shouldn't be too hard to find out. She's Dominic's granddaughter, recently moved here from out west."

"Can I ask why you're requesting a background check on the girl?"

"Because I said so."

"Excuse me, Mr. High and Mighty for daring to ask a question."

"You're not excused, but I'll tell you why I want the info since it might help. It looks like her ex-boyfriend has shown up to stalk her. From the sounds of it, he's a piece of work. Thinks terrorizing women is acceptable. I'd like to find him and show him why that's a bad idea." Show him in slow, agonizing detail why no one threatened those he considered his.

"You know murder is against the law," Hayder reminded.

"Only if they find a body."

"Good point. Do you have any kind of clue about this guy?"

"Not much. She used the name Gregory and

said they used to date when she lived out west. Oh, and she's got some kind of restraining order against him. He's also a wolf."

"A Lycan daring to come into our territory?" Hayder's tone changed. Arik wasn't the only one who didn't like encroachers.

"Daring and now threatening a woman. I want him found. I've given you enough details that you should be able to dig up some dirt. I want a picture of the asshole and more details."

"I'll have something on your desk in the morning."

Morning was too far away. "You'll have something for me in the next hour."

"You don't pay me enough for this," Hayder grumbled.

"I let you live. That's reward enough."

With Hayder's task set, and his anger still simmering, next Arik called Leo. "If you don't want the news to have a report of a lion running wild in the city, get your ass over here. And bring a bottle of cleaner and some rags." He rattled off the address before hanging up on his omega.

While he waited for Leo, he did his best to control his raging beast. But while he kept the lion contained, the man was pretty damned agitated too.

Someone had threatened Kira. She could tell him it was none of his business until the cows came to the kitchen door and offered themselves for dinner. Right now, she was upstairs. Crying. His feisty, outspoken mouse crying.

Like. Hell.

He'd respect her wishes to be alone tonight because he had work to do, such as making sure he didn't go on a beastly rampage—and peeing on every goddamn wall he could find so that if the wolf returned he'd know he'd incurred this alpha's displeasure. However, this was the last night they'd spend apart.

I've found my mate. And from here on out, she would never be alone again.

As soon as she'd come on his fingers, he was a goner. Human or not, Kira belonged to him, which would cause a shitload of problems, especially with the females in his pride. But he'd handle them. He was, after all, the boss—even if they tended to forget that at times.

Pacing the sidewalk in front of her building, he heard the hum before he saw Leo arrive on his fully decked out Honda Goldwing. Harley owners might stick their noses in the air at his choice in bikes, but only once had a pair of morons said something to Leo's face. Funny how the legend of him tying their beards in a knot traveled. Leo's version of poetic justice.

The big man got off his bike and strolled over to Arik, who had stopped to stare at the offensive door.

"That's not very nice," his omega remarked.

"Care to state something more obvious?" was Arik's snapped reply.

"Do I know who lives here?"

"Not quite, but you've heard of her and her cutting skills."

"I assume you mean the hairdresser. This is her door?"

"Yes, this is her door. She's upstairs right now crying because of the asshole who left this." Arik slammed his fist into the palm of his other hand.

"Judging by your current anger, I take it your

dinner date went better than expected."

"I would hardly call this better. I brought Kira home, expecting an evening of... Let's just say fun stuff, only to have her ditch me, terrified out of her mind because of some jerk."

"And you didn't kill someone?" Leo arched a brow. "I'm so proud of you."

"Keep your sarcasm. I called you here to keep me from doing something drastic. Your remarks aren't helping."

"If you feel a need to hit something, I'm here for you. And if it will make you feel better, I'll hit you back."

"I don't think that will be necessary." Arik didn't need to get personally acquainted with the pavement. Being alpha of his pride might make Arik strong, but when it came to brute strength, Leo outweighed them all.

The lion-tiger mix was a big bastard, but lucky for them, he had no interest in power or leading the pride. Leo loved his role as Omega, a guy who, with a single glance and crack of his knuckles, could calm any hotheaded situation. Or crack them together if required.

"I haven't told you the best part yet."

"The guy's a wolf. The blood scent kind of gave it away. Does she know?"

"Doubtful. But then again, I didn't really have a chance to ask her. If she's in the dark about our kind, then blurting, 'hey is your ex by any chance a werewolf?' is a sure-fire way to never have her see me again." As if he'd allow that.

"Again? The girl must have really struck your fancy."

She'd struck a lot of things. However, he

wasn't in the mood to discuss them at the moment. "Did you bring the cleaning supplies?" Arik asked.

"Yeah, but shouldn't we leave the message here for the cops? They'll want pictures for their report."

"She's not calling them." He could tell by the resigned way she'd even suggested it that she already knew it would do no good. The only thing she might achieve was having some disinterested officer take a report. In their eyes, this wasn't a true crime. Not until actual violence was dished would they get involved.

Violence. His lion heartily approved of it, but he'd have to do it in such a way that Kira wouldn't find out. He got the feeling she'd already faced enough.

Despite their short acquaintance, Arik knew Kira wasn't the type to get scared by petty threats, nor would she ditch her life to start over unless something truly bad had gone down. Nothing short of life-threatening would have Kira reacting the way she had.

He was proven right less than an hour later.

Hayder's voice didn't hold even a smidgen of humor when he called and relayed his findings. "I got what you asked for, dude. And it wasn't easy. This Kira broad might be Dominic's granddaughter, but they have different last names. Even once I figured that out, she wasn't easy to track. Your girlfriend isn't online with social media or anything. Lucky for us, I've got a second cousin on my mom's side who works for the cops out west. He was able to use his access to enforcement databases and he got a hit on her name."

"And?"

"And is Leo there?" Hayder stalled, which

didn't bode well.

"That bad?"

"Depends on how you look at it. Seems her ex-boyfriend was quite busy. At least according to her. Nothing concrete was ever proven, despite the many police reports and investigations. Seems Gregory has a history of leaving not-so-polite messages for Kira to find. She called the cops a few times for assault, but with no bruises to show for it, they never laid charges. I suspect Gregory had friends on the force. But even they couldn't cover his ass when he accosted her at work. According to witnesses, he showed up and went on a rant. She told him to leave, but he wouldn't listen. Numerous people claimed he shook her before shoving her against a wall. It was after that a judge granted her a restraining order, which prevents him from coming within fifty yards of her and, in addition, lists her residence, her parents' home as well as her place of business."

"In other words, the asshole is having a hard time letting go."

"More than hard. The restraining order just pissed him off. Things escalated after that. He attacked her outside her home, gave her a black eye, and might have done more if a passerby hadn't intervened. That got him tossed in the slammer for a few days, and more charges were filed, but they let him out on bail. It was while he was out that the salon she owned and worked out of burned down. Despite Kira insisting it was him, the investigator didn't find any concrete evidence linking Gregory to the incident. No accelerant was found, and the cause was attributed to rats chewing the wiring. Without hard evidence, though, the cops wouldn't book him."

And so she fled.

"Do you have a picture for me?" So Arik could see the face of the man he'd kill. Terrorize his woman? Not happening. Not to Kira. Scum like that did not deserve to breathe the same air as everyone else.

"I've got a few images. I'll text them over in a second."

"Good. After that, I want you to hire some security."

"The human kind or are you coughing up the extra dough for the Pack?"

Pack, as in Lycans who charged a hefty price for their services. Problem was while the Pack was the better choice, he didn't want any of those randy mutts sniffing around his woman. However, given they needed to protect her against one of their own, his jealousy would have to take a back seat. "Hire the Pack. But warn them they are not to have contact with her. I don't want her to even suspect they're watching. I want them for round-the-clock surveillance on her apartment and where she works. We don't want this asshole repeating his arson."

"Do you want a security detail on her?"

"No. I've got that covered." That was one protective detail he intended to handle himself.

With Kira, only the personal touch would do.

And as for Gregory… Arik left a message of his own should the wolf come skulking around again. An old-school message that had Leo wrinkling his nose and saying, "Did you really have to pee on her building?"

Well, yeah. How else was he to leave his calling card and take care of a pressing bladder all at once?

Chapter Twelve

Gritty-eyed and her body aching from a night spent on the floor, it was all Kira could do to drag herself down the steep stairs. She dreaded going out. Out meant too many places Gregory could hide and accost her from. Out meant seeing that vile message again, a message her uncle would spot when he came in to work. A visible threat that would require explanation.

If only she could stay hidden and pretend none of this was happening. Except ignoring it wouldn't make it go away. But she could hide away. This time, she wouldn't flee to a place with family. She'd go somewhere new, somewhere no one even knew her name.

This time I'll truly start over. Like she should have done in the first place.

She should have known better. In her stupidity to escape quickly, she'd put her family in danger. It wouldn't happen again.

She'd leave as soon as she got her paycheck from the barbershop. Once she cashed it, she'd come back for the bag she'd packed and call a cab for the airport. She'd hop on a plane to the first cheap location she could find. And once she got there, she'd board another plane to further muddle her trail.

The cowardice of running stung, but the fear

of seeing her family hurt proved stronger than her shame.

Since the fish shop would be open, her uncle an early riser, she took the inner set of stairs to go down, putting off the sight of the bloody message waiting on her exterior door. At the bottom of the steps, she paused and took several deep breaths. What would she say to her uncle? How to explain the vile note left on the door?

Or could she duck out while he wasn't looking?

From the safety of the storage room, she peeked around the doorjamb that led into the store. Her uncle argued with the radio as the announcer relayed sports scores and news. When he crouched down to wipe out the inside of the glass display case, she darted by.

"Morning, Kira," he said, his voice muffled by the glass. "What happened to your door?"

She didn't reply, just flashed him a wan smile and didn't stop. Her uncle deserved an answer, but she wasn't sure she could tell him without bursting into tears. Being a nice guy, he would insist on helping, and that would make things worse because then he might get drawn into the drama that was her life.

Best to run. She pushed open the portal to the sidewalk, only hyperventilating a little as trepidation suddenly filled her.

What if Gregory is waiting for me? Barely a foot outside, she froze as she glanced around.

The sidewalk proved bare of stalkers, just regular run-of-the-mill pedestrians. It all seemed so normal, so benign. The hand buried in her purse didn't loosen its grip on her can of mace. She wouldn't be caught unprepared.

Steeling herself, she glanced at the door that spelled the end of her short-lived, new life. Only the nasty message wasn't there.

She blinked and looked again. Still nothing.

Tacky, fresh paint met her fingers as she touched the pristine white surface of the door, and she could see her own reflection in the sparkling clean glass.

A shadow loomed over her. "It might still need another coat."

She let out a sharp scream, as Arik seemed to melt out of nowhere. How a man his size could sneak up on her baffled.

"Someone really should put a bell on you," she muttered.

"But then you'd know I was coming."

"What I'd like to know is what you're doing here."

"I wanted to make sure you were all right. After your abrupt departure last night and the unpleasant incident of the graffiti, I was concerned."

If she were a Popsicle, she might have melted. As it was, her knees went a little weak. "That's sweet, but as you can see, I'm fine, and I'm guessing I owe you thanks for getting my door painted."

He waved a hand. "No thanks necessary. The message offended me. So I took care of it."

"Well, whether you want any or not, thanks. It was nice of you. Now, if you'll excuse me, I need to get to work."

"Busy day of appointments?" he asked. Leaving his car at the curb, he matched her steps as she took off up the sidewalk.

"Not quite."

"In that case, why don't we stop in for some breakfast at the coffee shop across from it?"

"I can't."

"Lunch?"

She shook her head.

"Dinner." He stated, didn't ask.

She stopped and turned to face him. "Listen, Arik. You're a nice guy and all, and last night was real fun, and if I were staying, I'd—"

"What do you mean if you were staying?"

Funny how he got this weird, growly tone in his voice when he got upset with her.

"After what happened, I can't stay here. I'm leaving. Today. Probably within the next two or three hours. As soon as I can get my paycheck cashed, I'm heading to the airport."

"To go where?"

She shrugged. "I haven't figured that part out yet. I figure the less I plan, the less chance my ex will find me."

His brows drew together. "You're running because of him?"

"It's the safest thing for me to do, not only for me but the rest of my family."

"It's dumb."

Starkly said, and she felt the sting of the rebuke. "To you maybe." To her, it was the only plan that made any sense and kept her family out of harm's way.

"You're not thinking clearly. Running isn't going to make this guy go away."

"If I'm not here, he'll have no reason to stay."

"Or, if he can't find you, then he'll go after your family and try to make them divulge your location."

"He wouldn't—"

"What? Hurt them? Threaten them? Do you know that for certain? Are you really willing to take that chance?"

She clamped her lips shut as his reasoning filtered. How dare he poke holes in the only plan she had?

His voice softened. "I'm not trying to scare you, Kira. You've obviously already been through enough. But let's be honest here. This asshole is desperate. Desperate guys do unpredictable things."

"So what do you suggest I do? Stay here and hope I don't end up a blurb in a newspaper? *Hairdresser's body is found, victim of psycho ex-boyfriend.*"

Arik's eyes flashed golden as they caught the morning sun. "I won't let him hurt you."

A bitter laugh built of frustration left her lips. "And how will you stop him? You can't stay glued to me, twenty-four-seven."

"Want to bet?"

Funny, he sounded utterly serious. But she was a stranger to him. A no one. A CEO of his stature had better things to do than babysit a hairdresser. "You're being ridiculous."

"I see nothing ridiculous about wanting to protect you. Actually, most would call it chivalrous."

They would, except she couldn't help but wonder at his motive. "Why do you care so much, anyhow? We barely know each other. We hated each other until dinner yesterday." A lot had changed since then, though. Now they didn't hate, but she couldn't exactly define what she felt for him, or he for her. Lust, yes. Intrigue as well. But more than that?

"You know what they say about hate."

Yeah, she knew, but surely he wasn't so

arrogant as to think she loved him, and she wasn't gullible enough to believe for a minute he loved her.

"This whole conversation is nuts. And I'm wasting time. I need to get moving."

"If you insist. Let me give you a lift."

"It's not far."

"No, it's not. However, given the possible danger to your person, you shouldn't go alone. So ride with me, or walk. It doesn't matter. Either way I am accompanying you."

"You are as stubborn as a donkey." She politely refrained from using the word ass, but more because it made her think of his tight butt instead of a braying animal.

"I prefer tenacious kitty."

Kitty? Arik had too much presence for anything so domestic as a cat.

"So what will it be, mouse? Are we walking, or shall I drive you in style?"

In the end, she chose comfort and immediately regretted it as soon as she planted her butt in the decadently warm passenger seat. The cab of his truck, while spacious, was still rather confined—and intimate. The scent of him, his cologne and general essence, surrounded her, teased her with memories of what had happened last night in that very same vehicle.

Staring at his hands on the steering wheel, she couldn't help but recall what those hands had done to her the previous evening. How he'd brought her such pleasure. The recollection flushed her, and a shiver went through her as desire throbbed between her thighs. It appalled Kira that her mind could so easily get distracted, especially at a time like this. She forced her gaze away.

Yet, that didn't diminish her awareness of him.

A good thing he didn't seem to notice. His eyes remained trained on the road, and he kept his hands—unfortunately—to himself.

Not in the mood to talk, she toyed with a loose thread on her jeans, not paying much mind to their route until she realized they'd driven for a while and not yet arrived.

She peered through the windshield and frowned. "Where are we? This isn't the way to the barbershop."

"No, it's not."

"Are you taking a roundabout way? Are you trying to shake Gregory in case he's following?" She craned to glance behind them, wondering if one of the cars tailing them held her ex-boyfriend. Was he even now plotting to ram them and turn them into road kill? Would he drive them off a bridge? Open fire? Or…

She slammed the door shut on her overactive imagination that ran through too many movie plots for a paranoid mind to handle.

"We're not actually going to the hair shop."

His words penetrated, and she diverted all her focus to Arik. His amber gaze briefly met her own, striking her anew with his good looks—and the smug smirk he wore.

"What do you mean we're not going there? Exactly where are you taking me?" Hopefully not to some deserted location where he could kill her and dispose of her body. With Gregory on the scene providing a likely suspect, perhaps Arik now saw his chance to get revenge for his hair. It wouldn't be the first time her poor judgment in men had led to her jumping from the frying pan into the fire.

She gave herself a mental slap.

Not all men are psychos. She somehow doubted that the CEO of a billion-dollar company was a closet serial killer. But she had to wonder at his plans when he answered.

"We're going to my condo."

His condo? Which probably meant a place with a bed and privacy. A comfortable location where they could pick up where they'd left off the previous night. Not exactly the most awful plan, and yet… "You can't be seriously thinking of seduction at a time like this. I realize you're probably still a bit blue balled considering how our evening ended, but really, what makes you think I'm in the mood to have sex?"

He laughed so hard the vehicle swerved, and she squeaked as she grabbed at the handle on the door.

"You think I'm taking you there for seduction?"

His incredulous tone had her frowning in annoyance. "Well, what else am I supposed to think? I tell you I need to go to work to grab my paycheck so I can leave, and you decide, without asking, to hit your bachelor pad. I fail to see your humor."

"For one, while we will most likely have sex, and more than once, the reason I'm taking you there is first and foremost for your safety. My building has excellent security, round the clock."

"And what's the other reason?"

"Isn't your protection enough?"

She shook her head.

"How about, I've decided to not let you out of my sight."

She couldn't help but ask, "Why?"

"Because you're mine."

Possessive. Stated matter-of-fact. And utterly unexpected.

She blinked and tried to process it. She failed. "Excuse me? Did you just say I was yours?"

"Yes."

She should have slapped him for his temerity, not want to melt and plaster him with kisses. She tried to shake the pleasure at his possessive words. "You do realize slavery was abolished. You can't own people."

"Who said anything about being a slave? I can promise, when you are mine"—she noted his use of when, not if—"you won't have any chores to do. I've got more than enough staff to cater to your needs. Well, except for any lusty needs. Those I intend to handle myself."

"So I'm to be your sex slave? How is that any better?"

"Mouse, you have some very messed-up ideas when it comes to men. When I say mine, I mean you're my woman. My mate."

"Um, that sounds kind of permanent. Not to mention a little fast. I mean, just yesterday, weren't you telling me how you wanted me as your mistress and weren't looking for a relationship?"

"I changed my mind."

"Only women get that prerogative."

"I'm the boss, some even call me king." He winked. "I can do whatever I like."

"Narcissist."

"Are we back to alphabet attributes because, when it comes to the letter N, I would have said neat."

"Neat? As in tidy or cool?

"Tidy of course. You'll be glad to know I'm

not a man to leave my socks on the floor."

"Because you have staff to pick them up."

"What's the problem with that? It's my neat side that makes me hire them to keep my place in spotless shape. I also have a cook so we always eat well, a tailor, and a massage therapist, who, on second thought, you can't use."

She stupidly asked, "Why not?"

"Because he's a man. No hands but mine are allowed to touch you."

Again, his possessiveness should have appalled her, but dammit, her attraction to control freaks once again reared its head. She tried to laugh off his jealous claim. "Oh my god. I'm stuck in a truck with a mad man." And a rich one.

As he slowed down under a covered portico supported on pillars of marble, Kira couldn't help but gape at the towering building. Story upon story of reflective glass that sparkled in the sunlight.

A valet sprang forth and opened the truck door on her side, but before Kira could grasp the gloved hand to step down, Arik was there, scowling at the fellow in the red uniform trimmed with gold braid.

"I've got her. You take this." He tossed his keys at the fellow. "Don't park it far. I might need it again quickly."

Tucking Kira's arm in the crook of his, he led her to a bank of glass doors, which were so clean they shone with mirror-like brilliance. Kira felt woefully out of place. Even the doorman seemed more impressive than her. She really wished she'd worn something a little more presentable than a comfortable pair of jeans with worn holes in one thigh and knee, a soft dusky rose pullover that had gone through the wash one too many times, and hair hastily slapped into a pony tail. Add to that the worn canvas runners on her feet, and she looked more like someone who should enter through the back entrance as a worker than a guest of one of the condo owners.

Dragging her feet didn't stop Arik from propelling her forward, his large hand firmly pressed against the middle of her back. She could have probably darted away, yet she had a sneaking suspicion he would just chase her down and carry her in, caveman-style. The man seemed bound and determined to protect her from Gregory.

And truthfully, at this point, bemused by the strangeness of it all, she allowed it.

Why not? What did she have to lose? Her methods hadn't worked. The cops hadn't helped. Moving half a country away hadn't stopped Gregory. Why not let Arik and his arrogance take a stab at deterring her ex?

Even if he failed, at least she'd get a moment to relax in comfort—and maybe enjoy some seductive pleasure.

Or she'd go from one bad situation to another. A prisoner with a gilded cage and a much-too-sexy captor.

Chapter Thirteen

Bringing Kira to his home was both brilliant and yet, at the same time, the height of foolishness. Arik knew it, but he did it anyhow. He had his reasons. Valid ones, too. For one, he wasn't exaggerating when he'd mentioned his place had the best security around, and he didn't just mean the actual paid-guard kind. No stranger would make it into the condo tower without someone in his pride noticing—and taking care of it.

That was the smart part of his choice. The foolish part, though, was exposing his human mouse to the females of his pride. Talk about throwing Kira to the lions. But it had to be done at some point. If Kira was going to be a part of his life, then best get her used to the insanity of his family from the get-go—before she discovered the even crazier fact that her mate and his relatives were shapeshifting lions.

Now there was a conversation he wasn't looking forward to. How did one spring the fact that he turned furry, roared, and liked to hunt gazelle, on a woman whose closest encounter with a large feline was probably at a zoo?

Maybe Hayder could find a how-to manual for him.

He'd worry about that later. First, he needed to run the gauntlet of the front lobby so he could get to his home. Home for him was the penthouse suite on the seventeenth floor of the towering condo complex. It should be noted that he owned the entire building and that the units were, for the most part, occupied by members of his pride. There were a few that he rented to friends of his, a mixture of humans and other shifter castes, but for the majority, it was she-cats. And they were all related to him in some shape or fashion, which meant he couldn't hope to sneak in with Kira and not have it noticed, especially since he made it a point to never bring his lady friends home, until now.

As soon as he stepped through those glass doors, from the comfortable couches and chairs set around an open gas-fueled decorative fire pit, lounging bodies perked with interest. Heads swiveled in their direction. Conversations stopped. Eyes followed their steps as they made their way to the elevator. Steps that slowed as Kira shortened her paces until she stood frozen.

"I don't think this is a good idea." She didn't look at him as she said it, but at the staring eyes of his cousins. "I don't belong here."

She did. She just didn't know it yet. "We can talk about it upstairs."

"Or I can just leave right now." She spun on one heel, determined to leave.

As if he'd let that happen. He sidestepped and blocked her. She moved the other way, only to have him block her again.

"Get out of my way. I'm leaving, and you can't stop me."

That made him laugh. "Oh, mouse, when will you learn you can't challenge me and hope to win? We're going upstairs, and that's final." The sooner, the better, as the lionesses were taking too much interest in their repartee, and some were beginning to close in, curiosity drawing them.

This argument needed to cease. He was the alpha—*king of my pride, hear me roar*—and he needed to act like one. Despite the gossip it would engender with his audience, Arik grabbed Kira around the waist and carried her to the elevator, which opened at his approach.

Lucky for him, none of the pride confronted him before he left the lobby. The not-so-lucky part? They told his mother.

But he wasn't aware of that fact for a whole three minutes. Three minutes he got to spend alone with Kira glaring at him in the elevator.

How cute she looked with her arms crossed under her breasts. He wondered what she'd do if he told her it just tempted him to rile her even more.

She'd probably take the scissors to me again. Problem was, while hair grew back, other parts of his anatomy wouldn't, so perhaps he shouldn't push his luck.

"You know, in some states, I'm pretty sure this is considered kidnapping."

In his world, the laws didn't apply unless he made them. "Isn't kidnapping like a female fantasy in romances? Dashing billionaire abducts lovely hairdresser so that he might do decadent things to her luscious body?"

"This isn't romantic. And there will be no decadent things done to *this* body." She gestured to her shape, drawing his eye to the curves he longed to explore.

"Oh, there will be things done. And you will enjoy it."

"No, I won't."

It was too easy to prove her wrong. He invaded her space, his body moving toward her as she backed away in the elevator cab until she hit the wall and had to stop. Her chest heaved, her eyes dilated, and the sweet perfume of her arousal teased him. "Care to change your answer?" he whispered, brushing a strand of hair from her cheek.

"Stop it. I know what you're doing, and I won't allow it."

"What am I doing?"

"Using your body against me. Just because I desire you doesn't mean I like you."

"I think you do like me. A lot."

"No, I don't. At all. Nothing. Nada. Zilch. Never in a million years."

He grasped her chin and rubbed his thumb over her lower lip and felt her tremble. "Again with the lying. And you protest too much. Admit it. You are as drawn to me as I am to you. And not just physically. We complement each other."

"How do you figure that? We are completely different people."

"Which is why we will work so well together."

"What is wrong with you? I insult you, and you think that makes us perfect?"

"But that's just it. You are not cowed by my evident awesomeness. Your fearsome nature makes you a perfect partner for me."

"You wouldn't call me fearsome if you'd seen me last night," she blurted out. As if ashamed of her admission, she ducked her head, but he wouldn't let her hide from him. He angled her chin and forced her gaze back to his.

"There are times when fear is appropriate.

When threatened, anything less would be foolish. But you aren't afraid of me."

"Because I know you won't hurt me."

The admission warmed him, made his chest swell in pride. Odd, because, with anyone else, he would have shown them why fear of the lion king was appropriate, but with Kira, he wanted her trust. "You're right. I wouldn't hurt you. Because you are mine."

Before she could protest, and he could tell she was going to, the stubborn chit, he slanted his mouth over hers, drawing her denial into his mouth and breathing arousal back into her.

Kira melted, just as he knew she would. This was meant to be. In his arms he held his woman, his mate. She molded herself to him and let his mouth trace the shape of hers. She met his tongue with her own, eagerly sucking and playing and…

The elevator doors parted, and a choked cough—someone had a meddling hairball stuck in their throat—let him know they had an audience.

"What do you think you're doing, Arik Theodore Antoine Castiglione?"

Ooh, all four of his names. Someone was in trouble. Or would have been if he were still a child. However, he was a man now. Alpha of the pride. What a shame his mother kept refusing to respect his command.

With a heavy sigh, he parted from a flushed Kira and turned to face his mother, who regarded him with stern disapproval from the open elevator door.

In her early fifties, his mother appeared much younger than her age, her skin still smooth, marred only by crinkles at the corners of her eyes. Her blonde hair, with a little help from a bottle, retained its golden sheen and was cut short in layers that framed an angular face. The lips, which usually bore a smile for her cherished son, were pulled taut in disapproval.

"Hello, Mother. Fancy seeing you here. I take it someone tattled on me."

His mother arched a perfectly plucked brow. "Make that numerous someones and with good reason. What are you doing bringing a hu—"—she caught herself—"a girl like her home with you."

Before Arik could say a word, Kira, being Kira, jumped in.

"A girl like me?" His mouse planted her hands on her hips and let her expressive brown eyes spit daggers at his mother. Fearless before the pride's greatest huntress. Except Kira didn't know whom she faced. *Even if she did, I'd wager she wouldn't care.*

It occurred to Arik to intervene, but he stayed his paw. This confrontation would have to happen at one point. Given both women would always be a part of his life, Kira and his mother would have to learn to deal with each other.

That was the first reason to allow this meeting to unfold. The second he could blame on his cat, who was curious about what would happen next. Fireworks for sure and he wondered if he could snag some popcorn for the upcoming entertainment. His mother wasn't used to other people, most especially humans, standing up to her.

Haughty disdain marked his mother's features as she eyed Kira from head to toe. "Exactly where did you scrounge this waif from? The bargain bin at some discount outlet? Really, Arik. If you feel a need to sate your carnal urges could you not do so more discreetly or at least with someone of your caliber?"

In other words, stick to his kind, not humans.

But Kira didn't know that. Kira assumed the worst, and she bristled pretty awesomely—for a human.

"Having met you I see where Arik gets his manners, or, more specifically, lack of manners, from. I have to wonder if the fumes from the peroxide you've used over the years on that pile of straw on your head is to blame."

"It's natural!"

"Sure it is." Kira's placating smile just fueled the fire.

"Why, you little hussy, I should teach you to mock your betters."

"Mock? I'm sorry. Wasn't my insult clear?"

Oh damn. What a way to goad his mother. Arik could see his mother's control over her lioness fraying. Since it seemed the claws might come out, he judged it prudent to step in.

"Now, ladies, surely we can solve our differences in an amicable manner."

"No!" At least, in that, his mother and Kira agreed.

"Can we go inside and discuss this?"

"You and your mommy can. I'm leaving." Kira, who'd yet to exit the elevator cab, made to stab at the touch screen, but Arik blocked her attempt.

"You're staying," he stated.

"Let her leave. It's the first smart thing she's said." His mother glared at his mouse.

"Kira's not going anywhere."

"You can't make me stay."

At this point, Arik finally lost his composure. He might have let his cat out just a tiny bit when he roared, "Enough!"

Round eyes and a dropped jaw said he might have let a little more beast out than expected. While

Kira processed her shock, he took the opportunity to extract her from the elevator and carry her to the door to his penthouse. His mother followed, haranguing him all the way.

"What are you doing, Arik? Why are you bringing this woman home? I want some answers."

There really was only one answer, and he tossed it at his mother before slamming the door practically in her face. "She's mine."

The roar of denial from the other side of the wooden portal didn't bode well, but then again, neither did the storm brewing in Kira's eyes when he set her down.

Guess he wasn't getting any nookie or a nap anytime soon. Damn. And the sun was at just the right height to puddle warm rays across his bed.

Chapter Fourteen

The harpy, masquerading as Arik's mother, left, but her accusations still rang in Kira's head. But the fact the harridan took an instant dislike to her wasn't what perturbed Kira so much. Rewind to Arik's manhandling of her. It took her a moment to process what he said but once it sank in, she had to ask, "What the hell was all that about?"

"I'd apologize for my mother's behavior, but to be honest, that's just how she is."

"I don't give a damn about your crazy mother. I'm talking about the whole 'she's mine' bit. I'm really starting to get a little perturbed by this whole caveman thing you've got going on. You don't own me, big guy. I'm not some bauble you can just claim and then tote around." Even if said toting was kind of hot. "I'm the one who gets to decide where I go and with who."

"Not at the moment you don't. You're in danger, so you won't be going anywhere for the moment. Not until this problem with your ex-boyfriend is taken care of."

"And just how do you plan to take care of Gregory?" Because short of her ex getting distracted by some other poor girl or getting his ass thrown into jail, she couldn't see how Arik thought he could help her.

"Let's just say I have my ways."

The toothy grin didn't reassure, not with the cold storm brewing in his eyes. "You aren't going to kill him or something, are you?" she asked, only half joking. Something about Arik said he wasn't a man who did things in half measures. But surely, he wouldn't stoop to violence or murder? Then again, what did she really know about him?

"Would you care if Gregory were to meet an unfortunate end?"

What an odd question. "If you're asking if I care what happens to Gregory, then no." The violent jerk deserved anything that happened to him. "But that scumbag isn't worth getting in trouble for. Not to mention, I don't think orange is your color, and you're not the type of man to bend over for soap. So let's keep things legal. In other words, no hiring any hit men or putting Gregory's feet in cement and throwing him off a pier."

He laughed. "You really have a vivid imagination. Hiring hit men." He snickered. "No need to worry on that score. I'm more a hands-on kind of guy."

And what nice hands those were. Big. Strong. Distracting. "Keep your hands clean. Gregory isn't worth getting arrested over."

"I wouldn't get caught."

The cocky reply had her rolling her eyes. "Your arrogance really knows no limits. Just stay out of it. Please. I don't need your help."

"And yet you're getting it anyhow."

Frustration bubbled over, and she let out a screech. "Why are you being so stubborn?"

"Because I like you."

Way to suck the irritation out of her. She

blinked at him, noted for the first time since he'd abducted her this morning that he still wore the suit of the night before, albeit wrinkled, and with the tie hanging loose. His jaw glinted gold with the rough start of stubble, and lines of fatigue creased his features.

The truth struck her. "You never left last night."

"Of course I didn't. Did you really think I'd leave after seeing that message and how frightened you were?" He stated it as a matter of fact, as if there was never any doubt he'd guard her.

The realization he'd stuck around, just to watch over her, wrenched at her heart. Here he'd done something utterly sweet, uncalled for, and yet so nice, and here she was being a right bitch.

And why?

Because he scared her.

Arik frightened her, not because she feared he'd harm her in any way, despite her accusation of him kidnapping her. No, she feared him because he seemed too good to be true.

Look at him. Rich, handsome, sexy beyond belief, totally interested in her, not at all daunted or put off by her stubborn attitude, and capable of handling her sarcastic tongue.

The perfect package—with the classic bitchy mother. He was every girl's romantic fantasy. But she didn't believe it. Didn't believe she could be so lucky.

There has to be something wrong with him. Something she didn't yet see, and yet the more he revealed himself and his personality, the more time they spent together, the more attracted she was.

She tried to push him away out of fear, but he wouldn't budge. He kept attempting to have her trust him. He demanded she let him protect her. He commanded all of her senses with just his presence.

He wants to make me his.

Was his devious plot working?

Hell yeah. She wanted to succumb.

But what if I'm wrong about him?

Could she allow herself to get immersed in his world and his life, only to later find out he was bat-shit crazy? Would he turn out to be as aggressive as Gregory when it came to being with her? What if she did allow herself to believe they could have a relationship, only to have him tire of her once the challenge was gone? Could her ego, and heart, handle that kind of rejection?

The real question was, did she dare take a chance that they did have something real between them? Or would she let past experiences and mistakes turn her from a possible bright and pleasurable future?

While she went through her mini epiphany, he yawned. A big, jaw-cracking yawn of epic proportions. She couldn't stop a giggle.

"I'm glad you think this is funny. I need a nap, but I daren't close my eyes because you'll probably bolt at the first snore."

"You snore?"

"Can I lie now and say I don't?"

The admission of this flaw only endeared him more to her. "What if I promised to not leave while you slept?"

He arched a golden brow. "This is priceless. Are you asking me to trust *you*?"

Ironic, she asked him to grant her the one thing she kept refusing to give him, a measure of trust. "I'm being serious. I promise to not leave while you're napping."

"I'd like to believe you, mouse, but you're tricky. How about a compromise? I'll nap if you join me."

"You want us to sleep together?" She and Arik in a bed, sleeping? Ha. As if her body would let that happen.

It seemed he came to the same conclusion. "On second thought, I don't know if I could sleep with you so temptingly close."

"It's a bad plan. I agree."

"I never said that. I might not be able to sleep, but I'm willing to try." He yawned again as she eyed him dubiously.

"Sleeping only. No hanky-panky," she reiterated. Although she had to wonder if it was more a warning to herself than him. He truly did tempt her. A temptation she would resist. They were both grown adults, capable of controlling themselves. *Hear that, hormones? I am in charge, and I say hands off.*

"If you insist." How dejected he sounded.

A part of her wanted to insist on the opposite. However, she could see the fatigue in him now that she truly paid attention. He wasn't the only tired one. She'd slept only in restless spurts the previous night. Still, though, she and Arik sharing a bed? She muttered one last feeble protest. "I don't have any pajamas."

"Would a T-shirt of mine work?"

Only a thin layer of cotton and her panties separating them? She'd have to make sure she kept to her side of the bed.

She changed in the bathroom, stripping out of her clothes to slide on the large T-shirt he'd procured from a walk-in closet. While freshly laundered, the fabric softener scent reminded her of him. Her soft sigh of pleasure made her grimace.

I am so pathetic. Unable to stop lusting after a guy who was so obviously wrong for her.

When she emerged from the marble splendor known as his bathroom—the enormous shower with its glass enclosure and bank of showerheads meant to massage tempting her for a quick dip—Arik was already under the covers, lying on his side, his back to her, head on the pillow. Sleeping already?

For a moment she debated grabbing her clothes and fleeing. Forget her promise. She knew this was a bad idea.

"Get your luscious butt into this bed, mouse."

Stupid mind reader. "What makes you think I wasn't? We made a deal."

"Yes, we did, but I get the impression that you're now getting cold feet. Are you going to run like a scared mouse from me?"

She should. In some respects, he frightened her more than Gregory because, with Arik, she could truly see the wondrous possibilities—if he was being real.

Given how wrong she'd been, though, about her ex—make that a string of failed boyfriends—she no longer trusted her own instincts. But, at the same time, she wasn't a coward, and she wanted to keep her word. "A deal is a deal. I'll sleep with you, but what about when we wake up?"

"Then all bets are off."

What the hell was that supposed to mean? She didn't dare ask.

She made her way around the massive king-sized bed. It didn't look out of place, though, in the luxurious bedroom. Decorated in a very masculine color palette comprised of ebony-stained wooden furniture, the space featured a bed with a tall, carved headboard with a matching tall boy dresser, night stands, and a bench covered in plush blue fabric poised at the foot of the bed. The walls were painted a dove gray while the shag carpeting, which her toes curled in with delight, was a deep blue. His comforter was done in shades of gray and white, with the pillows more the hue of a dark stormy sea.

It was all male, very expensive and surprisingly comfortable. Clambering onto the mattress, she sank a little in the pillow top but didn't go sliding on satin sheets. While extremely soft, the white sheets caressed the exposed parts of her body.

"What kind of material is this?" she asked, rubbing the fabric to distract from the fact she currently lay in bed with Arik.

"Bamboo with some kind of ridiculously high thread count."

"It's nice."

"And you're trying to bore me to sleep. Nice try." An arm snaked around her waist and drew her across the smooth surface of the bed. She squeaked then sucked in a breath as she came to a stop cradled against a distinctly male, and very naked, body. Make that an aroused body.

"Um, I think you forgot something, big guy."

His words emerged muffled, probably because he nuzzled the hair at the back of her head. "What?"

"Pajamas? Maybe some track pants. Underwear at the very least?"

"I sleep naked."

Of course he did. She couldn't really claim surprise, however… "That's great, except you're kind of not alone. And given the plan is to nap, kind of distracting." Make that arousing. Hopefully he wouldn't notice the fact that her body heated like a bajillion degrees, his proximity igniting her desire for him.

"Do I distract you, mouse?" The warm words tickled the nape he'd exposed.

She shivered. His lips pressed against the skin, a tender erogenous zone that shot warmth into her body. "You are supposed to be sleeping," she protested.

"Just getting comfortable," he purred, the sound vibrating on her skin.

Comfortable? How could anyone claim comfort with something hard poking at her backside? How could she hope to sleep with a delightfully heavy arm cradling her, holding her close? How could she think to relax with the heat of his body wakening all her nerve endings, and his warm breath teasing, and his scent...

Screw this.

She made a noise as she squirmed to turn around.

"What is it?"

"Oh, shut up." This time, she was the one to silence him. She kissed him. Kissed him knowing full well what would happen next. And it was his own fault.

Stupid, sexy hunk of a man.

Kira wasn't dead. Or blind. Or incapable of desiring. A part of her fully understood she barely knew the guy and that things were completely messed up in her life. But, dammit, a girl could only take so much.

Or she could take it all. Take what Arik kept teasing her with.

He didn't protest as her mouth nibbled at his. He didn't push her away when her hands explored the breadth of his shoulder or the brawny length of his arm. He complied completely when she pushed him onto his back and she slid atop him, body to body, her legs parted to allow the stiffness of his shaft to stand straight. His rigid length rubbed against the moist crotch of her panties, a tease that had her clenching muscles.

"What happened to napping?" he murmured as her lips left his to explore the stubbled edge of his jaw.

"I need something to relax me."

"Are you using me?" he asked in mock indignation.

"Totally." Kira wasn't some wilting flower when it came to her sex life. She didn't always need a man to seduce her. And what was more delicious than seducing a man of such power like Arik?

"Oh, mouse, you are unique." He breathed the words against her lips, having drawn her face back to his.

In one swift motion, he rolled them, placing her beneath him, the tip of his shaft pressing against her still-covered sex.

Her breath caught, and yet her heart raced. He braced himself on his forearms and let his mouth travel. Down from her lips to the smooth skin of her neck. Nibble. Lick. He stopped at her pulse, which surely throbbed, and he sucked. Each tug of his mouth sent a jolt to her sex.

How it heated her entire body. The moisture of her arousal made her slick, her panties so wet.

He left the spot he'd marked and moved lower, his jaw brushing over the swell of her breasts, dragging at the soft material of the T-shirt.

She hated the fabric that separated them. Wished it would disappear. Then didn't think at all as his mouth caught the erect nipple protruding through the cotton.

Hot. So hot, and pleasurable. *My god.*

The material soon became soaked as he sucked at the tip of her breast, managing to tease the nub and heighten her arousal.

She cried out when he abandoned this erogenous zone but then gasped in anticipation as his destination became clear.

Down. Down. Down her body he traveled, his touch blazing a trail down to the edge of the T-shirt, which had ridden up to her waist during their antics.

He placed a soft kiss on the round swell of her belly. But didn't linger.

Down some more he moved, even as her breath grew ragged and her fingers clutched at the sheets.

He reached the edge of her panties and caught at the elastic hem. He tugged it with his teeth, dragging it down over one side of her hip. She couldn't help but glance down as he did it and could have swooned at the image he presented.

Crouched over her, his eyes smoldering with lust—*for me*—his teeth gripped the fabric of her panties.

He held her gaze and yanked some more at the fabric. She sighed. So hot.

So in the way.

Or so she thought.

With a savage yank and a growl, that was utterly too sexy, Arik tore the panties. Turned them into a useless scrap that no longer impeded his access to her.

Which suited her just fine.

He hovered between her thighs, his hot, panting breath fluttering against her exposed sex. She quivered. She couldn't help it. She also squirmed, her hips trying to invite him to get closer.

He did. His lips brushed at her nether lips, rubbing against them.

She jerked, her lower body bucking, bringing those lips in sharper contact.

A rumbling laugh shook him. "You are delightfully impatient."

Try delightfully aroused and in no mood to wait.

Thankfully, neither was he. The tip of tongue lapped at her sex. Then again. Each stroke grew bolder, longer, more satisfying.

He parted her sensitive lips and tongued her, teasing flesh. It was wonderful. It heightened her desire. It…paled in comparison when his tongue found her swollen clitoris.

Forget lying still and basking. The electric pleasure when he flicked his tongue against her had her bucking off the bed. He pinned her down, a heavy forearm across her hips all he needed to make her a prisoner to his decadent oral ways.

She cried out, the sounds breathy, incoherent, but encouraging because he didn't relent. On the contrary, he seemed determined to drive her insane with bliss.

He drew her close to the edge. She hovered on the brink.

He stopped.

She whimpered. "No. No. Don't stop."

"I'm not. However, this time, I intend to feel

you when you come," was his gruff response.

Feel it how?

Oh. *Oh*. The fat head of his shaft found the entrance to her sex. It pushed, thick and slick with her juices. Her thighs opened wide to accommodate his body. He slid in with decadent slowness, drawing out the pleasure of him stretching her channel, filling her completely.

He sank to the hilt and stopped, the rigid length of him pulsing within her. Her sex pulsed in reply, fisting him tight.

He groaned, and she opened heavy eyelids to see him poised above her, his head thrown back, the cords of his neck taut. Because he held his body braced above her, she could peer down and see where their bodies joined. Flesh to flesh.

A sound escaped him, a guttural expression of need and impatience. She peered at his face to find him staring at her. Eyes glowed a molten gold and, in a trick of light, or because of the passion glazing her sight, appeared less than human.

But utterly captivating.

Their gazes remained locked as he began to move, a slow, steady cadence that brought him deep, so deep, then withdrew until only the tip of him touched. Then slam, back in with a quick thrust that made her gasp. Shudder. Squeeze.

Again, and again, he did this to her. Slow retreat. Fast thrust. Pure pleasure.

With a scream, she climaxed. She gripped his shoulders tight as she did, nails digging into his skin. But he didn't seem to care as he pistoned her shuddering flesh. His head dipped until his lips rested against the hollow at her throat. He sucked at the skin as his body pumped, drawing out her ecstasy, wringing a second orgasm from her that had her screaming mouth wide open, and yet not a sound emerged.

When he came, it was sudden. His body tensed and thrust deeply, one last time. Mouth open wide over the fleshy part of her shoulder, his teeth pinched the flesh, hard enough she would have yelled if she had breath.

But the pain was fleeting, the pleasure overwhelming, and the sated stupor that came after too relaxing to fight.

This feels right.

She didn't even protest when he rolled them so that, once again, she lay spooned against his body. Nor did she move away when he nuzzled her hair and softly whispered, "Mine."

Chapter Fifteen

Arik woke before Kira did and took the moment to study her.

In repose, all the lines of worry eased. She didn't bear the tension of fear, the crease of confusion, or the taut lips of contrariness. For the moment, she appeared at peace and, given the slight curl at the corner of her mouth, content. *Because I pleasured her.*

And he'd pleasure her again. Often.

It was his intention to ensure she wore this look all the time. Well, maybe not always. He did so enjoy it when her fiery nature took over. How attractive she was when she went on the attack, her eyes snapping, her posture aggressive, and her chin tilted stubbornly.

Absolutely gorgeous. But most beautiful of all was her passion. The way she'd seduced him only hours before had proven beyond glorious.

They would do well together. Better than well. Even though she lacked a felidaethropy gene, she held great strength. It would serve her well in his pride. As alpha, he needed a mate who could hold her own.

However, just in case she needed more than words to defend herself, he should probably arm her as well. A sharp tongue could use a sharp knife just in case the claws came out.

Something he'd deal with later. First he wanted to—

Bang. Bang. Bang.

—kill whoever knocked at his door.

If Kira weren't slumbering, he would have roared at whoever dared disturb him. Wait. She didn't sleep. One eye crept open, and he saw the moment she realized where she was and with who. A happy smile pulled her lips. The heat radiating from her body increased. Her bottom squirmed against his groin. A certain part of him stirred and said hello. A shared desire sparked their bodies.

Bang. Bang. Bang.

The knock came again. Insistently.

"Bloody hell," he yelled as he rolled out of bed. "Can a man not enjoy a nap in the middle of the day?"

Let's go rip whoever disturbs us into shreds. His lion had ways of dealing with people. Unfortunately, they were kind of messy.

"Answer your door," Hayder yelled, no longer content to just pound his door.

"What if I don't want to?" Arik bellowed back, even as he stomped, naked and uncaring, to the entrance of his condo. He'd long ago confiscated keys to his place. Not because he didn't trust Hayder, but more because his damned mother kept having copies made. The sly lioness would enlist his cousins into tricking Hayder so they could borrow and copy them.

Now he used a thumbprint. *Duplicate that, Mother.*

Bang. "Dude, what is taking you so long?"

"Ever think to use a freaking phone?" he snapped back as he slapped his thumb on the touch screen display.

"I did, but someone was too lazy to answer it."

"No respect," Arik muttered as he flung open the door. He planted his hands on his hips and barked, "What the hell was so important you had to come disturb me?"

"You're the one who said to contact you if that dude surfaced."

Instantly all thoughts of killing Hayder and crawling back into bed with his woman vanished. The alpha returned, and he cut the bullshit to go straight to the point. "What happened?"

"Not much since the security we hired headed him off, but that Gregory dude tried approaching her apartment."

"Did the security team apprehend him?"

Hayder shook his head. "No. Something spooked him off before he got close enough. One of the guards said he took a big sniff then took off running."

Of course he did. When Arik marked something, lesser predators knew to scatter.

"Did they not give chase? Did you not tell them I wanted this guy captured?"

"Yes and yes."

"But?"

Hayder shrugged. "They lost him."

Nothing could stop Arik's snort. "Lost him? I thought we'd hired professionals. What did they give us, untrained pups? So much for their reputation as the best. You tell Jeoff, when you speak to him, that I am not impressed."

He did so love to needle the leader of the Pack. It was something they'd been doing for years.

"Tell him yourself. Jeoff is downstairs in the

common meeting room. I somehow didn't think you wanted him coming up here while you were *napping*. And I didn't dare leave him in the lobby with your cousins. There are more of them milling than usual."

Probably because word of his guest had gotten around. Also, who knew how much drama his mother was spreading? When it came to rumors and rabble rousing, she was the pride's queen.

"Tell that mangy wolf I'll be down in a few minutes. I need to locate some pants." Meeting with Hayder naked was one thing. His beta had seen him in the buff many times and didn't require impressing. But dealing with other alphas meant he needed to project a certain aura, one that didn't come with a swinging dick—even if he was impressively endowed.

"Pants would be good. A shirt too. And remember, there's no time for *napping*," Hayder chided, his implication clear—and unwelcome. "Also, you might want to think about hopping in for a quick shower."

Wash the scent of his mate from his skin? No. Yet, at the same time, he didn't want to share the sweetness of Kira's lust with anyone else. *It belongs to me. She is mine.*

Even if she'd probably protest it.

Annoyed with his beta, for many reasons, the key one being because he couldn't *nap*, he slammed the door shut in his smirking beta's face.

It sucked he wouldn't get to relax a little more with his woman. He could have used another dozen or so hours of sleep—and, yes, the rumors were true. Felines did enjoy their slumber. But now was not the time to nap. Given Gregory had tried to make a move, and that Kira would worry about her family, he needed to get out of here and act.

Oh, and he should probably do something about the sixty-three texts flashing on his phone, all from one slightly psychotic person, the one who'd birthed him after forty-seven hours of hard labor, who gave up everything for him—the everything which had yet to be defined—the bane and most important person in his life—until he'd met Kira. His mother.

Upon entering his bedroom, he noted the empty bed. He inhaled deeply, catching the lingering fragrance of their lovemaking.

Can't we spare a few minutes?

He really shouldn't. But even if he couldn't seduce his new mate, he should find her, which didn't prove hard. He followed the sound of water to the bathroom. Upon entering, he stopped and leaned against the doorjamb, admiring for a moment the delicious image meeting his gaze.

He'd located Kira. She stood within the shower's glass enclosure, getting soaked by the rain head pouring on her. He knew she saw him enter, the quick flick of her eyes his way noting his presence. However, she did nothing to hide the splendor of her curvy body. It glistened, wet and tempting.

Hands, slick with soap, slid over the moist skin, cupping full and heavy breasts, skimming over the indent of her waist, caressing the rounded shape of her hips.

But it was when that soapy hand reached between her thighs that Arik snapped. He stalked to her, glad he didn't have to waste time stripping.

He knew what would happen when he got in that shower. Knew it. Wanted it. *Will have it. Have her.*

A part of him understood he was out of control. He didn't care. He would take her, now, in the shower. He couldn't wait to hear her cry out. But, at the same time, he'd get clean. Pleasurable multitasking. Even Hayder couldn't find fault with his excellent time management skills.

And he knew Kira loved his climactic skills.

A brilliant smile met him when he stepped into the wet enclosure.

"Hey there, big guy," she said, her voice husky. "About time you joined me."

"Sorry for the rude awakening. I had some business to tend."

"Oh, are you going to have to leave?"

"Yes." *Meowr.* So sadly uttered.

"A shame." Soapy hands, hers of course, skimmed over his chest and moved lower. Lower. He swallowed as she gripped him and stroked. "I was kind of looking forward to using you to wake up."

"And does this using resemble how you used me to fall asleep?"

Her mischievous grin widened. "Yes. It's an amazing cure for lots of things."

Utter perfection. And his. Even if she didn't know it yet. "I don't really have much time. I've got a business associate"—with horrible timing—"waiting for me."

"This doesn't have to take long." Her hands stroked his erect length.

No, it wouldn't take long if she kept touching him like that. "You deserve more than a fast rut in the shower."

"What if I want a quickie though?"

How could he disappoint his mate? He would do this one thing for her. Ha. Great justification. "I guess I could manage something quick."

"I like *quick.*" She gripped him tight on the last

word, and he groaned.

He crushed her lips, kissing her with a fierce passion that hadn't lessened one bit. On the contrary, he felt more enflamed and desirous of her than ever. She bore his mark. She was his mate. His woman.

He would have pressed her against the wall of his shower so he could drop to his knees and please her. However, the massaging jets didn't leave much space. And she did want quick.

The question was, though, was her body ready for him?

As he kissed her, he let his fingers quest south of her waist, trailing through the wet curls of her mound to the tender flesh between her legs. She gasped against his mouth and arched her hips toward him.

Aroused, yes, but was she honey-wet within?

He slid a finger in. Gushing moisture met him. Hot flesh pulsed around his finger. Her hands clutched at him, frenzied.

He seesawed the finger in her and noted the shudder that swept her body.

So ready for him.

And he for her.

He withdrew his hand and swallowed her whimpering cry. He spanned her waist, reveling anew in her hourglass shape. All woman.

With brute strength alone, he hoisted her and whispered against her lips, "Wrap your legs around my waist."

She did, quickly and without a word. It locked her core against him, just above his shaft, which bobbed just below her bottom.

He tugged her slightly away from him and angled his hips, positioning the tip of his cock against her core. Lightly, he pushed, inserting himself with agonizing slowness.

How tightly she clutched him.

How hotly she enveloped him.

How deep she took him!

She locked her ankles around him and flexed, drawing herself against him and sheathing him the rest of the way.

Their lips clung together, hot breaths meshing as he flexed to thrust, in and out. She wrapped her arms around him, almost as tightly as her legs. Her body thrummed with tension, a live wire ready to snap.

He well understood that feeling. He wanted to snap too.

Faster, he thrust, a body-to-body grind that stimulated her G-spot, which, in turn, meant her channel quivered and squeezed, fisting his shaft.

He could have stayed in that pre-climactic moment forever, but she came. And came hard.

She screamed into his mouth, tightened all around him, and her sex shuddered and spasmed in waves of bliss.

It was too much. Too wonderful. Too... *Aaaah.*

He might have roared the wordless sound. Thankfully, she didn't seem to notice as she hung limply in his grasp, her head resting on his shoulder.

Cradling her in his arms, Arik enjoyed the moment. A moment that went on for a while until he felt compelled to ask, "Are you okay?"

She stirred against him. Her head tilted far enough for him to see the lazy smile she shot him. "Better than okay." She wiggled in his arms, and he let her down, hiding his smug satisfaction as she wavered on wobbly legs, a smugness that faded when she said, "That sure beats waking up to Frosted Flakes and milk."

Did she really compare him to— "Processed cereal?" He shuddered. "Don't tell me you eat that stuff."

"All the time. I like it. It's fast and easy. Who doesn't like a bowl of sugar to perk them up in the morning?"

"Not me. A lion needs real food."

"Lion? Someone's got a messed-up opinion of himself," she teased, not realizing his verbal gaffe. "Although I'll admit you do kind of remind me of an animal with some of the noises you make."

If she only knew those noises were just the tip of his furry, perfectly tufted tail.

"So sue me for being a man who expresses himself vocally when aroused. But I warn you, sue me at your own peril. I have the best lawyer in town on retainer."

"If you ask me, your money would be better spent with a psychiatrist for your ego problem."

"Admit it, my supreme confidence is sexy."

"No, it's disturbing, but lucky for you, your butt is awesome."

He might have blinked as she both insulted and praised him at once. He didn't know if he should pounce on her and nibble until she apologized or pounce and nibble to thank her. Funny how one solution worked no matter the scenario.

Problem was, any scenario would have to wait. He had business to attend to.

Meowr. Yeah, the man was disappointed too.

"So, does your dislike of processed food mean there's nothing in the fridge?"

Beer. Coconut milk, which he preferred to the pasteurized cow kind. Utterly disgusting. As far as he was concerned, the only thing cows were good for was a thick steak, barely singed and slapped on a plate loaded with carb-laden side dishes.

Food. His tummy rumbled. This was a need he could take care of. He'd call the kitchen and have them whip up two breakfasts, actually, three. He had to remember to take care of his mate now too. "If you can hold on about fifteen, twenty minutes, then I'll have a proper meal sent to you while I'm at my meeting." Which he really needed to get to before Hayder returned with a chainsaw to cut through his door.

His beta was excellent at keeping him on track. The bastard.

The water still ran hot, and steam fogged the air. He grabbed the soap to perform a quick wash, at least that was his intent. Kira didn't make it easy, not when she ran her hands over the soapy spots, a teasing grin on her lips and a cock-hardening excuse of, "Let me help you get clean for that meeting you need to get to."

She was going to help him lose his mind, and given how dirty his thoughts were when she borrowed the soap and bent over to scrub her toes, no amount of cleanser in the world could help.

I need to leave. Now. Before he got distracted again.

Some days it sucked being the city's Alpha.

With a hard kiss and a groan of true regret, he left Kira in the shower and snagged a towel. He dried himself as he entered his closet to look for clothes.

When he exited a few minutes later, properly dressed in a suit, with an impeccably wound tie, he found Kira lounging on the bed, wearing only a towel.

Just a towel between him and—

Such a bad kitty.

Time to put aside thoughts that involved licking, biting, and scratching and to get to work.

The quicker I get done, the quicker I'm back here.

"I'll return as soon as I can," he promised, unable to resist running a hand down her leg.

She sat up and hugged the towel to her chest, not that it did much to hide her cleavage. "What am I supposed to do while you're gone?"

Tell her not to escape because she wouldn't get far? Forbid her from contacting anyone so she wouldn't compromise her safety? Should he tell her to not play with herself and save herself for him? Wait, that was only something women did in horror movies before the killer showed up. *I should order her to think of me.* On second thought, no need. *As if she won't be thinking of me.*

Kira was right about one thing. Arik was arrogant enough to know thoughts of him would plague her. Whether those thoughts were good or not, totally different question. "Why don't you take the time I'm gone to relax? Get a good meal in you. I'll have food sent up to you from my private kitchen." Not so private given most of his family used it too, but as alpha, he got priority.

"Sounds good. Have a good meeting." Cheerfully and only missing a June Cleaver, '*dear*,' to make it picket-fence perfect.

It was also completely out of character.

Almost to the door, Arik paused and turned to face her. "You are taking this way too well."

Expression innocent, she met his gaze. "Whatever do you mean?"

She didn't bat her lashes, but it was close. His brows drew together in suspicion. "You're pretending right now, aren't you, that you're okay with all this."

"Me, pretend?" Such wide, guileless eyes and... Ooh, the towel slipped. Yummy. Berries.

Eyes on her face. Eyes on her face!

He diverted his gaze and fought to regain his train of thought. "I mean this morning you kept trying to escape and telling me how you liked me but couldn't be with now. Yet now you're taunting me with your delicious body." Her smile blinded him. "And you're tempting me with promises of delights for later." She licked her lips. "And apparently want me to believe that you're going to stay here."

"Isn't that what you want?"

"Well, yeah. But I didn't think you'd agree so easily."

"Would it do me any good to argue?"

"No." And, yes, he realized his flatly worded reply probably made him sounded irrevocably cavemanish. He didn't care. He didn't want her going anywhere. Not without him.

She rolled a bare shoulder. "If it won't do me any good to argue, then what's the point? You've already proven you're bigger than me. Besides, I'm starting to appreciate the perks." She winked, and the towel accidentally slipped again. He almost tore off his tie and pounced.

Bang. Bang. Bang.

Damn Hayder and his awful timing.

Stupid responsibilities. They just had to come knocking at his door when he was thinking of knocking at her door.

Distracted again and, judging by her amused smirk, on purpose.

"Behave," he said, shaking his finger.

"That's no fun."

"Kira." He said it with a warning tone that his pride knew to listen to.

Except Kira wasn't one of the pride. "Oh fine, I'll be a good girl." Her husky laugh didn't reassure. "You be a good boy, and just so you know, I'll be thinking of you while you're gone," she threatened as she rolled onto her back, the towel riding up her thighs, parting at her hip.

He took a step her way. Stopped. Growled. He forced himself to turn away from the pretty pinkness he knew waited for him under that towel.

"Later. And you'd better be here, or else," he warned as he left.

Left with the image of her splayed on his bed. Ready and willing. Alone.

Grrrr.

Thus it was, with a little more irritation than Jeoff probably deserved, that Arik stalked into the meeting room.

"How the hell did you lose the target?" Arik snapped as he dropped into a sturdy leather-covered chair.

"Good afternoon to you too, *Your Majesty*." Jeoff's smirk went well with his sarcastic lilt. A man in his early thirties, Jeoff was alpha to the city Pack of wolves. While strong in character, he was no match for Arik and didn't have the strength or numbers to make a run for title of city alpha—or concrete king— which put him under Arik when it came to power.

Unfortunately, when it was just the two of them, his old school chum didn't always show the proper respect. If he hadn't liked the guy so much, Arik would have torn open his stomach, spilled his guts, and fed him to the sewer rats.

Stupid friend, first ruining his naptime and now starving the local rodent population.

"It was shaping up to be a great afternoon until it was interrupted by incompetence."

"Which is why I'm here in person to offer my apologies. My guys majorly fucked up, and they got an earful about it."

"So what happened?" Arik asked, somewhat mollified by the apology.

"The lone wolf we're hunting isn't just willfully ignoring the Lycan laws. He's also wilier than we gave him credit for. Given what we knew of his behavior, we expected someone erratic, easy to spot and corner. I mean, a guy dumb enough to think he can come into our—"

"Our?"

"Your city," Jeoff corrected without pause, "and threaten violence, especially against a woman, has to be working with a few loose screws."

"You expected a rabid?"

A rabid being a shapeshifter who'd let their animal consume their humanity. Perhaps they'd spent too much time in fur, or their psyche wasn't strong enough to control the beast within. Whatever the reason, their thinking was often irrational—to a human—unexpected, and violent.

"Even if he were a rabid, that doesn't explain how he evaded your men. I paid you guys to be on the lookout for him."

"And they were. However, he didn't smell like a wolf. The bastard doused himself in body spray. Add in a shaved head so he didn't look like his pictures, and the fact he carried grocery bags. My boys didn't clue in. It wasn't until they noticed he stopped at the corner of the building and took a big whiff that they realized who he might be. But by then it was already too late. He dropped the groceries and took off running. The guy is fucking fast. He lost us on the subway platform. He mixed into the crowd, and with all the various scents muddying the trail, we couldn't find him."

Much like Kira had lost him in the market the day they met. For the first time, he could see the benefits of living more remotely, where the human trails were few and a lion could hunt his prey.

"So he knows we're on to him." Not exactly the best news. Gregory would either fade into the background and leave Arik with no one to punish, or his next move would prove more subtle and difficult to detect. Arik needed to draw his attention before the coward went after someone more fragile and human, like Kira's family. Once he and Kira mated, their safety became his responsibility.

"You're keeping men posted on her apartment?" Even though Gregory probably wouldn't return, Arik preferred to keep the bases covered.

"Yes, and my guys are also closely watching her family and their places of work. If he surfaces, we'll nab him."

"You'd better."

"You seem awfully concerned about this guy," Jeoff stated. "More than a disobedient lone wolf merits. Has he hurt someone in the pride?"

"In a sense. He threatens my mate."

That was one way to stun an opponent.

"You? Mated? You have my condolences."

Arik frowned. "What's that supposed to mean?"

"It's always sad when a man gets shackled to a

ball and chain. Next thing you know, you'll be taking ballroom fucking dancing, calling everything 'ours', losing your closet to shoes, and having to watch romantic comedies instead of going to the bar with the boys."

"I'll also be having incredible sex multiple times a day."

"You could have had that without having her shackle you."

"I'm the one who claimed her."

"Why? Why would you do that?" Jeoff shook his head. "Don't come crying to me when she makes you wear an ugly sweater at Christmas."

"I won't cry because I'll make sure you and I have matching ones, given to you publicly, so you can't refuse. I'll have Hayder take a picture, and I'll post it on every social media site I find."

"You're an evil king, Arik."

"Thank you." He couldn't help a smug smile.

Jeoff laughed. "On another note, I need a favor."

Arik arched a brow. "A favor? It must be important if you're actually begging me for something?"

"It leaves me with a bad taste in my mouth too."

"Are you sure it's not the brand of dog food you eat?"

"Ha. Ha. King of the jungle, but definitely not of comedy. Seriously, though, this favor is important. I need a safe place for my sister. She's leaving her current pack, but not without difficulty. They've promised retaliation if she dares."

"They can't hold her if she wants to go." The current laws prohibited it. So long as another pack promised to take them in, a shifter could move. It hadn't always been that way. In older times, the only way to escape was by marriage, a complicated treaty, or death.

"These guys are a rough bunch. But her mate died, and now that he's gone, she doesn't feel safe."

"Why not protect her yourself?"

"Because I can't afford to start a war. The last alpha of this region, as you well know, decimated the pack with his petty squabbles. I don't have the numbers to stand against these guys. But my sister needs to leave. I figure if she's here, surrounded by your family and under your protection, they won't dare to attack."

And if they did, they'd regret it. A lion's pride was sacrosanct and so were those adopted into it.

"I'll give your sister safety. However, I will expect progress on this wolf running about my city."

"Done."

They shook to seal the deal, and then they exchanged a few more pleasantries, which only served to heighten Arik's impatience to return to Kira.

Jeoff finally took his leave, but Arik wasn't so lucky. A pair of feuding twins arrived, spitting and meowing at each other, and demanded he settle a dispute—Krista had borrowed her car and left a scratch. But Korey borrowed her favorite blouse and stained it.

Ridiculous squabble. They both got dish duty for the week in the kitchens. No dishwasher allowed. Hand wash only.

That would teach them to waste his time.

But they weren't the only ones.

Each item only served to delay his return to Kira.

Sweet Kira. He wondered what she did in his absence.

Chapter Sixteen

As soon as the door to the condo shut behind Arik, Kira sprang into action.

How right Arik was to suspect she seemed too biddable. As if she wouldn't try to escape as soon as the opportunity presented itself. Kira wasn't one to sit back and let a man dictate.

Did she feel bad about lying? A little, although she hadn't fibbed when she told him she appreciated the perks of being with him.

As a lover, Arik proved amazing. The man oozed sex appeal and didn't disappoint. She had a happy body to attest to that.

However, great sex, sizzling chemistry, and an unfathomable like for the guy didn't mean she'd just bow down and turn into someone she wasn't, uttering, "Yes, master, anything you say, master."

It seemed they shared one trait in common, stubbornness. Kira also possessed a strong sense of responsibility that meant she wasn't one to let others solve her problems.

She'd heard enough of his conversation at the door to know Gregory hadn't left town or given up on his vendetta. From the sounds of it, Arik's security detail had scared him off from her apartment, but what about the barbershop? Her aunt's pizzeria? Her uncle's fish store?

It occurred to her to call and check on her family. However, she didn't see a phone in the bedroom. Arik did, however, have a touch screen inset in the wall, which, when tapped, told her in a dulcet female voice, "Unrecognized facial pattern and fingerprint. Main menu entry denied."

Wouldn't it figure the jerk would have the most innovative technology? How she missed the days of corded phones, and, of course, the cell phone she dug from her purse was dead. Again. She really hated how the darned things required constant charging.

Foiled when it came to contacting anyone, Kira spun on her heel and headed to the bathroom, tossing the towel to the side on the way.

She wanted out of here, but first things first; she needed clothes. The pile she'd folded on the vanity before the nap was still there if somewhat humid from the steamy shower. She didn't care. She dressed quickly in her things, cringing only a little at pulling on the underwear. They were still fairly fresh since she'd worn them only briefly that morning.

Peering in the mirror, she grimaced at the unsightly mess she presented. A rummage of the vanity drawer netted her a hairbrush, and from within her purse, she scrounged up an elastic. It took only a moment to bun her wet hair, a necessity because she couldn't bring herself to face the world with scraggly wet strands hanging in her face.

Ready to leave, she faced a dilemma at the door exiting the condo. A tug on the handle showed it was locked. There was a keyhole, however, that required a key, or lock-picking skills that she didn't have. She eyed the touch screen alongside the portal. She didn't expect it to work, but she tried anyway, tapping the surface. The stupid control panel chirped its irritating message.

"Access denied."

"Argh!" She didn't hold in her scream of frustration. Locked in. A prisoner even if Arik hadn't done so intentionally. Then again, he probably would have done it on purpose if he saw she intended to leave.

The man really had a Neanderthal streak when it came to a woman's place, and he seemed convinced her place was with him. She ignored the spurt of pleasure in favor of annoyance.

She couldn't remain here. She had stuff to do. People to check on. A man to thwart.

Pacing Arik's living room, a sumptuous man cave of ridiculous dimensions, didn't soothe her anger. She ignored the most enormous television screen she'd ever seen in her life. She stared unseeingly at the polished bamboo hardwood underfoot. She avoided running into the large and curved, leather-wrapped theatre seating with built-in cup holders. She did pay slight attention to the enormous pillow on the floor that was currently bathed in bright sunlight. Given the few golden hairs she noted clinging to the fabric, she had to wonder if he owned a pet—a rather large one, given the size of the animal bed.

Out of the blue, a female voice announced, "Access granted." With a click, the door to the condo swung open. Pushing a wheeled cart topped with silver-domed, covered plates was a young woman dressed in black slacks and a white button shirt.

"How did you get in?" Kira gasped.

"Through the door," the puzzled woman replied.

A door that mocked her attempts to open it. "But how? Who gave you access?"

"Arik did, of course."

"He's in the hall?" Kira couldn't help but crane to peek, wondering if he lurked.

The young woman laughed as she shook her head. "No. I meant he gave me a one time access when he ordered the food."

So it wasn't just Arik who could use the touchscreens. They could be programmed for use by other people—just not her.

"I've brought your breakfast, ma'am," the servant explained with a wave of her hand over the cart.

Room service had arrived, but more important than the food, the woman brought with her a chance for escape.

Kira strode toward her and the open door to freedom. "Thanks, but I've got other places to be."

The waitress positioned herself in front of the door. "I'm sorry, ma'am, but my orders are to deliver your food and not let you leave."

Kira halted by the service cart. "Oh. But I have an appointment I need to get to."

"Again, I apologize, but I have my orders."

With a shrug, Kira sighed and turned to the silver domes. "I see. I guess I'll have to wait for Arik then. So what's on the menu?"

The waitress moved forward and leaned to grasp the knobs of the domes, whisking a pair off to reveal the plate underneath.

Not that Kira cared, or spared it a glance. Before the waitress could react, Kira bolted past her to the elevator. It was still open, so she slid inside, only to find herself confronted by the damned touch screen again. How had she not noticed all this technology when she made the trip up? *Probably because someone was distracting me.*

Despite knowing it wouldn't do any good, she plastered her thumb against the screen. It asked her to identify herself.

"Screw you and your access denied," Kira snarled as the damned thing foiled her plot to escape.

"Come back," the waitress cried, having deposited the lids and coming at her with determination in her gait.

Kira banged the touch screen in frustration. Screwed.

Or maybe not.

The doors slid shut before the waitress could reach her. Was the tongue she stuck out childish? Probably, but she did it anyhow.

The elevator descended, and Kira watched the numbers as they lit up atop the door, only to groan in frustration as they stopped well short of her destination.

When the portal slid open, Kira pretended nonchalance, staring at her nails, which were in major need of a manicure, given the chipped state of her nail polish.

A pair of young women boarded, both blonde, their hair a wild, long mess in serious need of a hot oil treatment, a decent trim, and layers for proper shaping.

How she itched for a pair of scissors and at least ten minutes with each of them. But she wasn't here to dispense beauty advice. She was escaping a megalomaniac—with a hot ass and hotter kisses—so she could deal with her psychotic stalker ex-boyfriend. Talk about a more exciting life than a regular hairdresser should experience.

While she feigned disinterest, the new occupants didn't attempt to hide their curiosity.

The elevator began to descend again, and Kira did her best to ignore the other passengers. They, on the other hand, openly stared until finally Kira couldn't help but blurt our, "What is it? Why do you keep looking at me like that?"

To her surprise, they didn't deny their interest. "We're trying to see why Arik chose you."

"You know him?"

The query met with giggles. "Of course we do. Everyone who lives in the building does."

Everyone female at any rate Kira would wager, and not without a touch of jealousy. Then again, who could blame them? Arik's good looks mixed with his powerful presence made him impossible to ignore.

"So have you two been an item for long?" asked one of the girls.

"We just recently met," Kira replied.

"And he's already bringing you home to meet the pride."

Meet the who? Kira's brow furrowed.

"I've heard that's how it happens," the one with split ends replied with a sage nod of her head, which was at odds with the piercing in her nose and left eyebrow. "One sniff and bam. Mated for life."

Kira blinked. "Excuse me? I'm not sure I understand." She really didn't. Both of them alluded to things that made no sense. Perhaps the blonde hair wasn't natural, and the girls had sniffed more fumes than was healthy.

"I don't think she knows," the non-pierced girl said with a tilt of her head. "Oh, boy. Wait until she finds out."

"Finds out what?" asked the newest person to embark the elevator, which had slowed and opened on yet another floor.

"This is Arik's, um, *girlfriend*," snickered the one with the piercings.

"Really?" Amber eyes, much like Arik's actually, which also resembled those of the girls who'd first boarded, perused her from head to toe.

She resisted the urge to squirm.

"I expected someone...taller."

Again the sense that she was missing something tickled at Kira, but she really didn't care enough to pursue it.

When the doors opened again, finally onto the lobby, Kira couldn't exit fast enough, eager to leave the crazy company she'd just met.

However, they weren't as keen on letting her go.

Literally.

Piercing girl grabbed Kira by the arm and began tugging her toward the couches in the main lobby lounge area.

"Um, what are you doing?" Kira asked as she gently tried tugging loose. To no avail. The young lady had a firm grip, and she wasn't relinquishing it.

"You have got to meet the gang."

"I really don't have time for this. I have to go."

"Does Arik know you're leaving?" The question came from her friend.

"Why would his knowing matter?"

The girl laughed. "Oh, that's priceless. Wait until the others hear about this. Hey, Lolly, you gotta meet Arik's new girlfriend."

Several sets of amber eyes swung her way, and

Kira dropped any pretense of subtle as she tried to yank free.

And failed.

"Hey, I never did find out, what's your name?" Piercing Girl asked, oblivious, intentionally, at Kira's attempts to extricate herself.

A big sigh left her before she replied. "Kira."

"Cute name. I'm Zena, and this is my cousin, Reba. And that other lady riding with us was Aunt Kate."

"Nice to meet you, really, but I have to go."

"Sure you do. But you can't leave before meeting the crew. This will only take a minute, or two, promise."

Against her better judgment, but not really given a choice, Kira found herself propelled toward the avid gang of women lounging. And she did mean gang.

A ridiculous number of amber eyes locked on Kira, the freaky gazes mixed in with a few blue, green, and brown ones. Most of the women sported golden manes, but a few were of a darker mix, and one had a bright red crown of curly locks.

And they were all very unsubtle about their perusal of Kira from head to toe.

Zena pulled her right into the midst of the curious gazes and announced, "Hey, everyone, I want you to meet Arik's *girlfriend*. Her name is Kira."

The odd inflection didn't pass unnoticed, but she didn't know what it meant. Nor did she understand why so many noses began twitching. She'd showered, and while she didn't have any deodorant on, she wasn't sweating and shouldn't stink. Yet, there was no denying many of the women present were sniffing at her, and a few wrinkled their noses.

"No way," one of the older women stated, her face wrinkled in a moue of distaste. "I don't believe it for a second. His mother would never allow it."

"He did bring her home though," another mused. "He's never done that before."

"And is that his mark on her neck?"

Sudden silence descended as their glances honed in on the love bite Arik had given her that wasn't hidden by the collar of her shirt.

What she wouldn't give for a scarf, and a way to escape this really weird bunch. What was with this weird obsession with Arik and his sex life?

"It was really nice to meet you," Kira said as she took a step back. Then another. Only to stop as she realized she was hemmed in on all sides.

"How long have you been seeing each other?"

"Does he know you're trying to leave?"

"How did you meet?"

Questions fired at her from all directions. Daunted, Kira answered the easiest one. "We met at my grandfather's barbershop."

An "ooh" went through the crowd, along with more than a few giggles and smirks.

Zena ventured to ask, "Are you the one who cut the chunk out of his mane?" The question shut them all up, and silence descended as they waited for her answer.

"Yes, but in my defense, he was acting like an misogynist ass at the time."

Apparently this was the right answer because laughter erupted, some of the younger girls giggling so hard they fell off the backs of the couches. It didn't seem to bother them. They hit the floor with an odd grace and rolled in mirth.

"Oh my god, did you really? You should have heard him when he came home," Reba said, practically crying she giggled so hard. She adopted a deep voice. "My mane. My precious mane. She ruined it. Argh." Reba's arms wrapped around her middle as she doubled over, gasping for breath.

Kira bit her lip, trying not to join in the laughter. She did feel kind of bad about her actions. But it seemed the women around her heartily approved judging by their comments.

"About time someone took him down a peg. He was getting a little too big for his britches."

"What do you expect from a spoiled mama's cub?"

"If you ask me, he looks a heck of a lot better with his short haircut."

Yes he did, but Kira wasn't crazy about the fact that others had noticed it.

"Hey, since you're a hairdresser and all, do you have any suggestions on what I can do with this mop?" Reba clutched at her shapeless strands and gave her a hopeful look.

When it came to fixing hair, Kira couldn't resist. Not when the young girl was in such evident need of follicle help.

But it wasn't until a certain broad-shouldered hunk in a suit came striding toward her a while later, while she was in the midst of giving an impromptu trim to Lolly—the scissors courtesy of a knitting Aunt Polly—that she suspected the women of using a stalling tactic. They'd kept her occupied just long enough to tattle on her.

When she realized it, she dropped her scissors, whirled and made a run for the front doors. She didn't have enough time to escape the arms that caught her.

"And just where do you think you're going?" he asked.

He didn't find her answer of "back to jail" as funny as the women did.

Chapter Seventeen

Arik concluded his final meeting and was surprised to see that the lounging gaggle waiting to pounce on him outside the conference room had dwindled to nothing. Apparently, they'd heard of his ill humor and decided to handle matters on their own.

Which suited him fine. He was eager to return to Kira, who hopefully still only wore that towel or, even better, nothing at all.

Thus, he was less than happy when he got waylaid on the way to the elevator.

His teenage cousin, Nexxie, stood in front of the panel, arms crossed over a neon top that sloped off one shoulder. Her messy hair hung in jagged lengths, pink hanks, blue, green, purple. She looked like a rainbow had thrown up on her head.

"Move," he ordered, not wanting to deal with the petulant jut of her lower lip.

"I am not budging until you do something about her."

"I don't have time today for whatever drama you're trying to drag me into." He hoisted her and put her to the side so he could jab the touch screen and request the elevator.

"Make time. This is life or death."

Wasn't it always? "I'm sure you can deal with it."

"Usually I would." Nexxie held up a fist, and shook it for emphasis, only to let it drop as she added, "But then Melly said you'd probably have a problem with me messing up your lady friend's face, especially since she's human and all."

Instead of stepping into the open elevator, Arik froze and spun to face his cousin. "When you say lady friend, are you talking about Kira?" Which should have been impossible. He'd left her locked in his penthouse. Except he'd also had food delivered by a kitchen staff member. Would Kira have used that chance to escape? The answer was, in the words of his many teenaged cousins, a resounding, DUH!

I knew she was faking it. Scurried away at the first opportunity. Or so she'd thought.

We'll chase her down and show her who's boss. Nibble at her tender spots until she forgot about escaping.

"Is this Kira chick a hairdresser?"

He nodded.

"Then, yeah, that's her. And you gotta do something about her. Did you know she thinks I should cut my hair short? And dye it brown!" His cousin practically choked on the last word. "She has to be stopped."

A nerve in his jaw ticked. He bit his inner cheek. His lip twitched. It didn't help. He laughed.

Nexxie stomped her combat-boot-clad foot. "This isn't funny! That hairdresser wants to make me look respectable and pretty. It's just wrong!"

Finally, something he could use against his rascally younger cousin. "Then you'd better behave, or as your alpha, I'll order it done."

Her eyes narrowed, both challenging and doubting. "You wouldn't dare."

"I'm alpha. I would dare. And so would she. Or did you miss what happened to my mane when I crossed her?" He didn't elaborate on the fact that he rather liked his new appearance. Anything to keep this troublemaker in line was worth a small white lie.

Nexxie's sharp teeth worried at her lower lip. "What if I promise I'll stay out of her way?"

"You'll have to do better than that. You'll have to be on your best behavior to avoid the scissors." He held his fingers in front of her and mimed a snip.

She recoiled. "Behave how?"

"Let's start with better grades."

Her shoulders slumped as she sighed, "Fine."

"Good. Keep your paws clean, and I'll make sure Kira doesn't come at you with a blow-dryer and a brush. Speaking of whom, where exactly is my mate improving the hair situation of the pride?"

"The lobby. A couple of the girls caught her trying to leave, and when we asked if you knew…"

She'd tried to lie to felines and gotten caught. At least the women of his pride didn't seem out to harm her, merely detain her.

Which meant he'd face a livid Kira when he got back. But two could play the game of betrayal.

She'd tried to leave. She'd broken her promise, which meant payback for starters. And, second, she needed to recognize she was, *Mine*.

It was time she learned what that meant.

Time to show her who she's dealing with.

Time to reveal his inner beast.

Rawr.

Chapter Eighteen

Escape foiled.

Strong arms caught her.

"Let me go."

"No."

An unrelenting grip tossed her over a brawny shoulder. And not one person tried to stop him. On the contrary, most wore amused expressions or outright snickered.

"Put me down."

"No."

"Arik!" She practically growled his name.

"Have I mentioned how much I like it when you say my name like that? And I mean *really* like it." His purred inflection didn't leave any doubt as to what he implied.

She tried another tactic, appealing to the women she'd just bonded with over hair. "Are you guys going to just stand there and let him kidnap me again?" She caught Zena's gaze and shot her a pleading look.

But her new friend, with her chic feathered and layered do, just shrugged. "He's the alpha."

Which Zena seemed to think explained it all, but made Kira only more confused. What was it about Arik that all these women seemed cowed by him? Or, worse, were they under his thrall?

He no sooner set her on her feet in the elevator cab than she planted her hands on her hips and harangued him. "What the hell, big guy? You can't just tote me around like a sack of potatoes."

"Why not?"

"Because it's not done. I insist you let me go this instant."

"You promised you wouldn't leave."

"What else did you expect me to say once you made it clear your plan was to keep me prisoner?"

"Prisoner implies a cell and hardship. You can hardly call my penthouse with its amenities that."

"No, but the fact I can't leave does. A gilded cage is still a cage."

"One meant for your safety. Your ex has not given up."

At his admission, she froze. "What do you mean?"

"He tried to approach your apartment. And more recently placed a call to the barbershop seeking you."

"My family—"

"Is safe. I have men guarding them, all of them. This Gregory person will not get near them or harm them. But this just goes to show it's not safe for you out there."

Perhaps not, but she wasn't entirely convinced it was safe here with him either. Something was odd about the situation. From the way he kept trying to insist she belonged to him to the freaky way all the women she'd met downstairs seemed aware of him and not surprised by his actions.

What had she gotten embroiled in? Had she inadvertently stumbled onto a cult, one with Arik as its leader? It would explain a lot and prompted her to say, "I will not become a part of your harem."

Leaning against the wall of the elevator, Arik perused her, his amber eyes lit with mirth. "My harem?"

"You know, those women downstairs who all seem to think you're some kind of god who must be obeyed."

His lips twitched. "I wish they obeyed. For the most part, they like to drive me a little crazy."

"So you're not denying you're their leader?"

"Why deny the truth? They do answer to me. All of the pride does."

There was that word again. Pride. But somehow she didn't think he meant the sense-of-achievement kind. The way he used it was more like the lion version. A fancy word instead of calling them what they were, a gang or cult.

"Well, whatever you guys are, or whatever you worship, I don't want any part of it. I am not into freaky sex harems or weird religious stuff. So, if you don't mind, while I appreciate what you're trying to do for me, I'd still rather leave."

Brawny arms crossed over his chest. "No."

"I am starting to see how some sane people are driven to murder." She glared at him.

He smiled. The jerk.

She fought the urge to smile back. Told her knees not to tremble or else. Or else what, she didn't know, only that she needed to remain strong against his allure.

"Oh, Kira. There is so much you don't understand."

"Then explain it because I sure as hell am getting tired of feeling like I'm missing something." A giant picture puzzle where she had all of the pieces but was missing a key one, the piece that would make sense of all the rest.

The elevator stopped at the penthouse level, and the doors slid open. Since there was nowhere to run, Kira followed Arik back to his place but kept her distance from him, preferring to pace in front of the wide bank of windows. The stunning view couldn't hold her attention, not with *him* in the room.

He took a moment to shed his jacket and loosen his tie before he dropped onto the couch, making no pretense of the fact that he watched her.

Time for some answers. "So," she said as she planted her hands on he hips, "are you going to explain what the hell is really going on?"

"You are so delicious, mouse, when you get all feisty."

"Don't you start that flirting stuff with me. I want answers."

"And I want you." The smoldering intensity in his eyes went well with the sensual smile he hit her with.

She kept trying to be mad at him, to keep her mind on track, and then he said something adorably possessive and looked too freaking scrumptious. How was a girl supposed to fight his allure? Maybe by fighting back with the supposed sexiness he couldn't resist.

"You know what? I want you too, except it's hard for me to accept a man who is treating me like a fragile idiot who can't handle the truth."

"More like a fragile doll."

"Don't you dare compare me to a plastic sex toy that you can undress and is anatomically correct. Unlike a blowup doll, I will talk back because I am real."

His laughter emerged, loud and unabashed. "My god, mouse. You say the damnedest things."

And he found her funny. Not everyone grasped her, oft times, sarcastic and very pointed humor. He teased her but didn't get mad when she teased back. Another reason to like him. The jerk.

"Yeah, you never know what my mouth will do." As soon as she said the words, she caught his smirk. His wink. And should have expected his, "I know what I'd like it to do," but expecting it didn't stop her blush.

She shut her mind against the fantasy visual of herself, on her knees, a hand wrapped around his—

Out of the gutter, you dirty, dirty mind. She yanked her thoughts into another direction. "Why are you so determined to get in my pants? Why me? I'm sure you can get any girl you want to sleep with you. I don't understand why you have to bed me."

"Because you're mine."

As if that was all the answer she needed. "Sorry, but that just doesn't cut it. Why do you think I'm yours?" What did he see in her?

While Kira didn't lack for self-esteem or care what others said, there was a womanly part of her that wanted to know how he felt. To see herself from his point of view. What attracted him?

"Does it make sense if I say I both love and hate your argumentative nature?"

"So sorry, master. Would you like me to get on my knees and kiss your toes for forgiveness?"

"Would you?"

She snorted. "No."

A laugh rumbled. "I didn't think so. Another reason I like you. You know how to stand up for yourself."

"Except with Gregory." Why she admitted that weakness, she couldn't have said. Perhaps to show him that his image of her was flawed.

"Tell me about him. Why does he frighten you so much? Because I got the impression that not much did." He moved left on the couch and patted the open spot this created.

Feeling awkward standing over him, she perched herself on the buttery leather. Soft. So nice. She ran her hand over the material, intent on it instead of him. Only inches separated her from Arik, a fact she was only too aware of. She should move away. However, sliding herself over, even if only a few inches, or popping to her feet, meant admitting he had an affect. The man was cocky enough as it was. She didn't need to encourage him.

She noted him staring and realized he was waiting for her to answer. Talk about Gregory. What was there to say? "We went on a few dates. He got real intense real fast. Kind of like someone else I know," she grumbled with a pointed stare his way.

Completely unabashed, he smiled, wide enough to pop his dimple.

Gregory had a dimple too, and it didn't just come out when he smiled. Rage made it pop too.

"I am nothing like that dog." Such disdain for a man he'd never met.

"No, you're not. For one thing, you got me in bed, and fast too." A healthy sex life didn't mean she jumped into the sack. In the past, she made the guy she dated wait at least a month. Several outings and conversation helped her weed out those interested in one-night stands and guys who irritated her. She'd always followed that one-month rule, until Arik.

And the worst part was she'd do it again.

Something about Arik made her explode, set her on fire, and while it bothered her, she couldn't seem to help it.

Regardless of what it said, she slunk a few inches away. He noted but didn't remark on it, much too pleased with himself at her admission that he'd seduced her in record time.

"It's because you and I are meant to be."

"Well, Gregory thought we were too. But I knew pretty early on he was not the guy for me. But because he was cute, and insistent, I kept dating him."

"I never date. I take."

"Yes, I know, Captain Caveman. And, at one point, Gregory wanted a piece too. But I said no." Wrong answer, apparently.

"I am going to guess he didn't take the answer well."

"At first he did. Said it showed I had good morals. That I was a true lady."

"Not in bed you're not." The naughty words drew yet another blush.

The man had a knack for heating various parts of her. She ignored it and continued with her story. "I began to avoid his calls. Asked him to leave me alone. Told him I wasn't interested in him anymore. He got mad. Started yelling and calling me some nasty names." One which Arik had seen painted on her door. "The first time it happened, the next day he showed up with flowers, an apology, and a promise to never do it again. I accepted his apology but wouldn't go out with him again."

"Is that when the real threats started?"

She nodded. "Messages left on my windshield, notes pinned to my door. He wanted me back. He hated me. I was the greatest thing on this earth. I was the demon queen out to destroy the world." The highs and lows of Gregory's rants chilled her still.

"The asshole stalked you."

"Yup. And the police couldn't really do much about it. They could caution him all they wanted. No restraining order was keeping him away. He just got smarter about his stalking and didn't leave evidence behind that it was him."

"All kinds of small dick stunts until the big one. The fire."

She frowned. "How did you know about that?"

"I had you checked out." At least he didn't lie. It didn't mean she liked it.

Spine straightened, she looked him in the eye. "You did what?"

"I had you investigated. When I saw that message on the door, I could sense your fear. I didn't like it, and having certain connections, I decided to find out what I could about the jerk stalking you. The fire at your old hair shop was one of the facts that popped up."

"And what else did you learn?"

"That you have a sister who lives with your parents in your childhood home. You graduated with steady C's and B's."

Not exactly a model student. "I hated school. Let me guess, you were an honor roll star?"

"The finest a prep school could buy."

"Explains a lot."

"Do you want to know what else I found out? Do you recall a certain full moon at the age of nineteen?"

She almost groaned. Lovely, he'd read about the time the cops caught her and her best friend skinny dipping, high as kites on 'shrooms, giggling that they were mermaids. In their defense, they swam pretty damned good and could hold their breath for up to a minute. She stayed away from fungus after that incident.

"This study you've made of me and my life is kind of creepy, big guy."

"Only because you barely know anything about me, so let me rectify that. I am an avid lacrosse player. Love the color gray. Am a smoothie fanatic. You'll have to try some of my signature flavors. I enjoy watching sports. Follow the stock market. And I can't wait to make love to you again."

Blink. He tossed those words in with nonchalance. But she had a harder time pretending they didn't affect her. "Things are moving too fast." Way too fast. He kept claiming they belonged together, and crazy as it was, she suffered from the same belief too. Had they become infected by some strange virus or drug that made them crave each other? "I don't understand what's happening to me. Why I feel so strongly about you. It's not natural."

"That's often the way it happens when true mates meet."

"There you go with that mate thing again. You can't just up and claim me, big guy. That requires something like permission."

"Or fate. And that is what we are, mouse. Fated. True mates, destined to belong together until the end of our time. We are the human equivalent of soul mates."

She stared at him for moment, trying to digest what he'd said, but it still baffled her. Arik was a mature businessman, not one given to flights of fancy. He wasn't really going to try this line of BS on her, was he? "Oh, come on, no way you can expect me to swallow the fact that you believe in soul mates, or love at first sight."

"As strange as it sounds, yes."

"Fated? Really?" She snickered. "Please don't tell me that harem downstairs fell for that dorky come-on line." The irony didn't escape her that she kind of had. He'd spouted possessive and flirty things, and she'd fallen right into his trap—and his arms.

In her defense, the man was sizzling hot, and she really didn't regret the sex. As a matter of fact, even though he was completely freaking nuts, she'd do it again. Kind of like her addiction to chips and dip, the man proved irresistible.

"First off, those women aren't my lovers or part of a harem. That would be really unseemly given they're all pretty much related to me in some way, shape, or fashion."

"They're family?" She couldn't hide her surprise. Then again, hadn't she thought the eyes freakily similar to Arik's? Knowing they were family also put a whole new spin on their remarks. They weren't sizing her up as competition for Arik's affection. They were checking her out to see if she was good enough for him.

Poor guy. She knew how cousins could be. "I wish someone would have explained that earlier. Still, the fact you don't have a harem doesn't change my point of view. I think you're feeding me a line about the whole soul mate thing, which you might as well stop. If you want to have sex again, just say so." He could rock her world anytime.

"This is not a con to get you into bed. We both know all I'd have to do is kiss you and…" His sensual smile said it all.

"You just can't help yourself, can you?" She shook her head at his arrogance. An alpha male at his most extreme. Frustrating and yet inexplicably sexy.

She really should seek some professional help.

"You're right. I can't help myself. I'd heard of the pull when a male meets his mate, but never expected it would hit so hard and fast. You are mine, mouse. The lioness, if human, to my lion."

"Lioness? And things just went from weird to where's the hidden camera."

"I am a lion. Therefore, it stands to serve that my woman would be my lioness."

Kira gasped as the truth hit her. "Oh hell, don't tell me you're one of those guys who likes dressing up in those big teddy bear costumes? Do you have some fuzzy Leo the lion costume that you like to wear and then get it on? You'd better not be because, I'll tell you right now, I don't swing that way."

Arik chuckled as he stretched his arms across the back of the couch, the movement pulling his shirt taut and outlining a perfection her body remembered only too well. Her blood heated, and moisture pooled between her thighs. She crossed them.

Why did he have to be so nuts? Why did her curse with men have to strike with him?

"I must admit, mouse, your mind works in really wondrous ways. But let me clarify. When I say I am a lion, I mean real lion. As in I turn furry, have great big teeth, roaring kind."

Said with utter seriousness. He truly believed he was a lion. Which meant he was working with a few loose screws, which, in turn, meant he could be dangerous.

She shivered.

As quickly as fear tried to insinuate itself, it dissipated. No, no matter what Arik's fetish, she didn't get the impression he was a violent man. Yet that belief didn't quite curb all the nervous hysteria from her giggle. "Joke's over. Good one. Ha. Ha. Can we get serious now and talk about our situation?"

"But that's just it. We are. There is a lot about this world you don't understand, Kira. Mysteries you can't even begin to imagine and truths I will have to reveal. The first being my feline side. However, that doesn't mean you have to fear me. As my mate, I will never harm you or allow others to bring you harm. I will be your staunchest defender. Another promise I make is that I will be faithful. From henceforth, you will be the only one to feel my touch. And, in return, you will not touch another. I have jealousy issues."

"Jealousy issues. Dictator issues. Freaking a girl out issues." Kira wrung her hands, a part of her doubting every word he said, recoiling from it. However, another part of her, the girl who used to believe in romance and the concept of love at first sight, wanted to trust. Who didn't want to live and enjoy the kind of love Arik proposed?

But what about freedom?

"I can't be with a guy who keeps me locked up."

"Ah yes, your continued insistence that I am holding you against your will."

"Well, you are."

"Don't make me kiss you and prove you wrong. Actually, on second thought, please do. It has been much too long since I held you naked in my arms."

Was there a comeback for that kind of brazen challenge? Not a verbal kind at any rate. Her body, on the other hand? It shivered, it woke, and all her senses came alive, hoping she'd do or say something that would force him to act upon his word.

She used the facts to bolster her resolve. "Attraction to you still doesn't explain why you locked me in your condo."

"How about a lack of time to have you placed within the condo's security system? An issue I rectified in between meetings, actually. See, I trusted you to stay inside. I took you at your word."

She shifted uncomfortably. "How do I know you're telling the truth? Maybe you're just saying that to make me look bad?"

"Don't believe me? Then touch any of the screens. See what happens."

"You're trying to trick me. There's no way it will work because you never took a handprint or thumbprint or whatever the hell it is that you use to make that stupid thing function."

"Your signature was captured when you tried to use the screens while I was gone. So yes, I do have it and as I said, I programmed my system to accept your touch."

This time, she didn't hesitate. She moved immediately to the display by the front door. Casting him a glance, she expected to find him watching, poised to stop her.

Wrong. Not only did he not move, he didn't even look back at her.

He's lying. He didn't—

"Access granted. How can I *serve* you, Kira?"

The innuendo from the house system was evident, but that wasn't what made her mouth round in an O of surprise. "You programmed it to talk to me in your voice?" She couldn't help a note of incredulity.

"Do you like it?" He flipped on the couch so he faced her.

"It's weird." Everything that had happened since she'd met him was Wonderland weird.

"Yes, and there are more weird things to come. Such as the first time I show you my beast."

Not that again. What was with this insistence on him being a lion?

"If you're a lion, then prove it. Let's go. Show me."

"I don't think that's a good idea. Not right now."

"Why not? You keep saying you're some great, big, furry beast, so let's see it. You want me to believe, and I'm willing to, with some proof."

"You don't know what you ask, mouse, but since you insist." He stood, removing his loosened tie as he did. He unbuttoned his cuffs then the seam that ran up the middle. The entire time he stripped his shirt, he kept his eyes locked on her. Eyes that burned golden fire. Eyes that were unlike any other eyes she'd ever seen. Human eyes at least. But there was something about the pupil that was different. And grew even more different as she stared.

Great, soon he'll have me believing he's a lion too. Just because he had unique and amazing eyes didn't make him part feline.

His voice was deeper, more growly, when he spoke. "I should warn you that this might be disturbing to watch."

Disturbing to her libido as he kept peeling layers. The shirt hit the couch, revealing his muscled upper torso, the flesh as smooth and tanned as she remembered. *I remember running my hands over that skin, the ripple of his muscles when he flexed, his body moving atop me.*

She swallowed. "Maybe we shouldn't do this."

"No, let's get it over with."

His hand went to his belt buckle. It went soaring, a sinuous strand of leather. His fingers unsnapped the button. His slacks hung low on his lean hips, the vee of muscle leading...

Bang. Bang. Bang.

Someone pounded on his door and shouted, "Arik. It's me."

Frustration contorted Arik's features, and he bellowed. "Does no one know how to use a bloody phone around here?"

"You left it in the boardroom."

"On purpose," Arik muttered, almost too low for her to hear.

"Jeoff called. They think they have him cornered, which means get your ass out here if you're coming."

Him as in Gregory?

Whirling back to face her, Arik confirmed it. "I've got to go. It seems we might have located your ex. Will you stay here until I return, or should I tell the system to lock you out?"

"I'll stay." It wasn't a complete lie. A part of her kind of did want to stay. Another part snorted hell no.

"When I get back, we'll finish our talk, and I'll show you my lion."

Wait a second, maybe by lion he meant his... Her gaze dropped, only to see the smoothness of his chest inches away.

He'd crossed the room too fast for her to react. His arms came around her, drawing her to him while his mouth slanted over hers in a scorching kiss.

One touch. That was all it took. He was right. She couldn't resist. She didn't even think of protesting, just melted at his touch, embracing him back with a fierce hunger that made no sense, but felt so good.

Felt good until he broke the kiss off, the idiot at the door pounding again and yelling, "I'm leaving."

"I'm coming," snapped Arik before releasing her.

As he grabbed at his shirt, Kira rubbed her lips, their tingling swollenness making it hard to forget the simmering passion he'd stirred.

"What are you going to do with Gregory?"

In the process of slipping on his shoes, Arik paused and faced her, an almost feral smile tilting his lips.

"I am going to make sure he never comes near you again."

Well, that sounded violently unpleasant, for Gregory. She should protest, but given what he'd done, she rather wished she could watch. Maybe get a kick or two in herself, payback for what Gregory had done to her.

With a growled, "I'm trusting you," Arik left.

And so was she before he could revoke her access.

She pressed her ear against the door to listen and heard the murmur of voices. They were cut off abruptly, probably because the elevator door slid shut. She counted to sixty before she slapped her hand to the touch screen and winced in guilt as his velvety voice said, "Access granted." The door clicked open.

Out she went, only to stop dead before the elevator. Only one cab for this level and it was on its way down with Arik, or so she assumed as she watched the numbers tick slowly backward.

What about the stairs? She vetoed that idea before seriously considering it. Twenty flights of stairs and her lazy ass weren't happening. Foot tapping, she waited for the elevator to reach the bottom floor. It paused there, disgorging its occupants. Then it began to rise. She waited for it to stop, move, and then stop again before calling it.

She hoped the stop and go meant it had disgorged its passengers. If not, she might run into another ambush by his family.

Finally, the elevator reached her, the door opened, and Kira didn't hold in her groan of dismay. "Not you again."

"Are you still here?" asked the harpy known as Arik's mother. "I would have thought you'd have grabbed all the silverware and run by now. Or were you hoping for a bigger cash-out?"

Someone didn't think Kira was good enough for her boy, which irked. *Arik likes me, a lot.* The knowledge made her bold. "Oh dear, is someone having problems cutting the apron strings? Does someone have a Norma Bates fetish for her son?" Kira's smirk probably accounted for some of the mottling on the other woman's face.

She sputtered. "You are the most impertinent chit I've ever had the displeasure of meeting."

"And you are the clingiest, peroxided, straw-haired harpy I've ever encountered. What do you say I leave and we pretend we never met?"

For some reason, that made Arik's mother snap her jaw shut. "You want to leave."

"Well duh. I wasn't just standing out in the hall for the view."

"Does Arik know?"

"No, he doesn't, and I really don't care if he likes it or not. I don't think I'm ready for the kind of commitment he's asking for." Not to mention she wasn't sure she could handle a guy who thought he was a lion.

"You're rejecting him?" The woman seemed indignant.

"Think of it more as just admitting that we're not quite looking for the same thing right now. And why do you care? You should be glad I'm going."

The woman shook herself and straightened. "You're right. I am glad. Arik needs to settle down with someone more suitable for his lifestyle."

"Snob." Kira muttered the word as she entered the elevator and stabbed at the screen. To her surprise, it worked. A part of her hadn't believed it would, certain that Arik would have somehow blocked her ability to leave.

Surely she wasn't disappointed that he hadn't?

In order to avoid the main floor crowd, Kira had the elevator stop one level above. She exited onto a hallway that ran left and right. Each side had numbered doors, but there, at the far end, a door with a push bar and the bright red letters spelling Exit.

Twenty flights was out of the question, but one? One, she could handle. Especially since, if she remembered correctly, the door spilled out behind some potted plants right by the main doors to the building. She'd noted it while playing with the women's hair earlier.

At the bottom, she paused and took a deep breath. She pressed her ear to the door and listened. Nothing. Pure silence. Surely that wasn't right.

The place had crawled with women before.

Then again, it was later now, dinnertime for many. Or so her belly rumbled. She'd gone way too long without any food. It made her wish she'd grabbed something off that trolley earlier.

But she wasn't going back for a snack.

She listened for another thirty seconds, silently counted in her head.

Still utter quiet.

Easing it slowly open, Kira used the door as a shield to peer around its edge. Through the palm leaves of the potted plants, she noted the many empty couches.

As a matter of fact, the whole main floor appeared absent of life, except for the check-in desk, where a male guard in his late fifties sat playing with his smart phone and, just outside, the guy by the front door who stepped from his post to grasp the handle of a yellow cab that pulled up.

Seeing her chance, Kira slipped out of the stairwell and quick-walked to the door. She thought she heard a, "Hey, where are you going?" from the guy at the desk, but she ignored it and skipped out.

Hitting the pavement, she didn't pause, nor did she look at the doorman at all. She briskly walked away, moving faster and faster, probably because of the murmur of excited voices behind her.

Soon she was running. She made it down the curved drive of the condo to the sidewalk. It wasn't a busy place, and the cars trolling it at this twilight hour were few, the area too residential.

She high-tailed it, feet pounding pavement, and, to muddy her trail for possible pursuers, ducked in the first alley she saw.

She'd escaped. She'd done it. As she reached the far end of the alley, which spilled onto a busier seeming street, she couldn't help but think it seemed too easy.

At any moment, she expected Arik to recapture her and ask in that husky murmur of his, 'Where are you running to, mouse?'

Except when the arms did snag her, they weren't the gentle haven she'd come to expect. And the voice was a grating lesson in why she should have listened to Arik and stayed safe in his condo.

"Hey, bitch slut, about time you showed your cheating face."

Chapter Nineteen

The tip from Jeoff's men saying they'd cornered Gregory proved a bust. The mangy wolf had evaded them yet again. Worse, he'd made fools of them. The rabid annoyance toyed with the men tracking him by leaving a trail that led to a pile of his clothes, along with a great big, still almost steaming pile of insult.

The bastard taunted them.

But why? He surely had to know it was a bad idea. Arik wasn't king for nothing. Now that Arik hunted, Gregory's days were marked. *Because once I find him, he'll learn a valuable lesson about messing around in my city.*

Big emphasis on the when Arik found him, which didn't happen that night.

Foiled, not in a great mood, and a sense of wrongness nagging, Arik returned to his condo. An empty condo.

"She left!" He said it aloud, unable to stem his disbelief. How could she have left? He'd disabled her access to the panel. He'd known better than to believe her. What sane woman would stick around after a guy told her he was a lion?

But he'd anticipated that, and as soon as he hit the elevator, he'd logged onto the condo's security system and locked down her access. Yet, according to the log he pulled up, someone had tampered with his instructions.

"Mother." He growled her name, and just in time, too, as she sauntered from his kitchen, a martini glass in hand, several green olives floating in the bottom. "What are you doing here?"

"Can't a mother visit her son?"

"Not a meddling one who, for some reason, gave my mate access to the building after I'd revoked it."

"Oh dear. Was I not supposed to do that? I was just trying to make the poor dear feel welcome since apparently someone foolishly decided to dally with a human." Her lips twisted, and not because of the sip of her martini, extra dry.

"Kira is my mate."

"Over my dead body."

"That can be arranged." He said it quite seriously, arms crossed over his chest.

His mother didn't seem the least bit affronted. She casually took another drink from the fluted glass. "Such melodrama. I expect that from your younger cousins—my sisters are such ninnies when it comes to raising cubs—but you are the pride's alpha. You are king of this city and lord over those who inhabit it. Act like it."

"I am, and it's as alpha I'm stating you've gone too far. Kira is my mate."

"Not a very willing one."

"That will change as she gets to know me, which would have been a lot easier were she still here. Where did she go?" Because she sure as hell hadn't been in the front lobby. A lobby that was rather empty, as most of his pride had probably gone to watch an underground shifter-fighting ring. The

Ultimate Fur and Fang Throwdown came to town only once a month and proved a huge draw.

"How would I know where she went? I merely provided her with the means to exit. I didn't drive her to her destination."

And she didn't have a car. Arik suddenly didn't like where this was headed. "Do you know if she hailed a cab?"

Even as he asked, his feet were moving, a sense of foreboding forming a ball in his stomach. *Don' t tell me the whole Gregory-is-cornered thing was a ruse.* A wily and brazen one, yet it would explain the false trail Arik and Jeoff had followed. The rabid wolf had distracted his hunters while he went after his true prey, Kira.

The elevator wasn't moving fast enough and stalled a few floors down. His sense of urgency mounted. He couldn't stand still. He took the half-dozen strides across the short hall and slammed into the bar that opened the door onto the stairs. His mother followed, haranguing him, "Where are you going? Why the hurry?"

"Why the hurry? I'll tell you why. Because you foolishly overstepped your bounds as my mother and allowed my mate, a woman in danger from a rabid wolf, to leave the safety of my home. You put her in danger." He leaped over the railing as opposed to jogging down and hit the landing for the floor below with a thump.

"I didn't know she was in danger," his mother cried, her voice faint from her spot at the top of the stairwell.

"Doesn't matter." What did matter was Kira. Not knowing where she was had his inner lion pacing. Perhaps she was fine. Kira might have simply left and made her way safely to one of her family's homes or even her own. But his gut didn't believe it, and it proved right.

Less than a block away, in an alley stinking of wolf, Arik came across her purse and a note, a note that was short but to the point.

Cum to the wearhouse alone or she dyes.

A misspelled invitation to violence. How fun. And he knew just what to wear. Fur and teeth. *Rawr*.

Chapter Twenty

Kira woke up…and cursed.

There were times in a woman's life when she wished she wasn't so independent. So stubborn. So bloody stupid.

I should have listened to Arik.

But, no, like a ninny, just to piss him off, and because he wasn't the only one who could act contrary, she'd made the wrong choice. She thought she was smarter than him, that she knew better, but it turned out she should get her IQ tested because a lack of good judgment had led to her current situation, bound to a chair.

This isn't good.

A brief squirm of her body showed she wasn't going anywhere easily. Rope, the nylon braided kind her grandma used for her clothesline in her backyard, was looped several times around her upper body. Nothing fancy, certainly not *kinbaku* level stuff— which, for the uninformed, was a Japanese style of BDSM rope bondage, something she'd learned from an ex-boyfriend who'd expressed an interest in educating her. She politely declined.

Deviant bedroom acts aside, professionally tied or not, the rope effectively immobilized her to the seat. Good news, though, her legs remained unfettered. Kicking her feet, in petulance since she had nothing else in reach, didn't do much to help her situation.

Since she wasn't going anywhere, she took stock of her current situation. It resembled a low-budget movie set. The place appeared rather squalid. The dim lighting that filtered through high square windows didn't allow for deep scrutiny, just some basic generalities. Judging by their lofty position, along with the dusty concrete floor and, to either side of her, what appeared to be stacks of shipping crates, Kira surmised she'd found herself in some kind of warehouse.

Totally cliché, and had someone played an ominous soundtrack in that moment, she probably would have wet her pants. She knew how this went in the movies. Either the girl got killed, which she wouldn't put past Gregory, or the girl got rescued in the nick of time—not likely given the person who might have noticed she disappeared had no idea where she'd gone. And there went that dum-dum-dum soundtrack again.

A scuff from behind had her straining to see who approached. Even before he spoke, she could have rightly guessed. "Finally awake. It took you long enough. My fault. I forgot when I injected you with that tranquilizer I stole from the vet that you're human and a little slower to process drugs."

He drugged me? Well, that explained the prick she thought she'd felt before passing out.

"Doesn't it figure you'd need to knock a woman out to get her to spend time with you."

Too late to bite her tongue. Such a smooth move. Antagonize the guy holding her prisoner.

"Still as mouthy as ever I see, something I once planned to cure you of." As he spoke, Gregory stepped into her line of sight, and she wished she could say he looked evil. That he was a loathsome bastard to look upon. He was anything but. Even now, knowing what she did about him, she couldn't deny he was a handsome devil with ebony hair that flopped boyishly over his eyes, aristocratic features, and a lanky body. Good looking with a superb physique, and yet he left her cold. Psychopathic personalities tended to be a turn-off.

"How long was I out?"

"Just over five hours. Long enough for me to get bored."

Bored and doing what? A man who was prepared to drug a woman and kidnap her might not draw the line at other atrocities. She took a quick stock of herself, wondering if he'd taken advantage of her unconsciousness. If he had, he'd not left a clue. Her clothing remained intact, and she didn't note any kind of soreness or stickiness. Still, she couldn't help but ask, "Did you do anything while I was passed out?"

The corner of his lip lifted, twisting his grin. His laughter grated on her. "As if I'd touch your tainted body. Not now after you've been with him. To think you rejected me, but I see you had no problem saying yes to that mangy tomcat. I'd not realized you were holding out for someone with more money. If I had known about your lack of morals, I would have treated you much differently."

"Different how? By leaving me alone and creeping out some other girl? You made my life such a living hell I had to move. What worse could you do?"

"I could have shut your pie hole with my cock."

"You would have needed more than that to keep me quiet. I've seen the size of your hands and feet." Once again, her mouth got her into trouble, but she couldn't help it. Despite the fear, she found a spark of fight. *I'm not going to die as his subservient bitch.*

The fingers that gripped her cheeks dug into her skin and bruised. "Keep talking, bitch slut. We'll see how brave you are once I'm done with you."

"Get your hands off her." Bellowing, and kind of growly, Kira still recognized Arik's voice. He'd come to rescue her.

Naked.

She closed her eyes and opened them again.

Nope, she wasn't hallucinating. Arik definitely stood at the edge of a line of shipping containers wearing nothing but skin.

Sexy, but still, she couldn't help but groan, "Couldn't you have at least brought a weapon?"

"I did," was his reply.

She frowned as she stared at his empty hands. "I don't see it. What did you bring?"

"Myself."

So much for a rescue. But at least Arik meant well as he strode toward Gregory, who was…what the hell? Why was Gregory stripping?

His shirt hit the floor, revealing a well-defined chest with a dark vee of hair arrowing down. Gregory toed off his running shoes. Hands went to his waistband, and the athletic pants were shoved down, revealing tight buttocks and corded thighs.

It took less than a minute for him to face off against Arik, stark, raving naked.

What the hell?

Perhaps the drug Gregory had given her hadn't yet worn off. She must be hallucinating. How else to explain the fact that two naked men went into a half crouch, arms extended at their sides, and fingers flexing. They watched each other warily, treading in a slow circle, preparing to fight.

Gregory dove first, a flash of pale skin rushing at Arik's bigger, tanned form. Arik sidestepped at the last moment and put out a foot. Gregory didn't fall, but he did stumble.

"I see you got my note," Gregory stated as he pivoted back to face Arik.

"How could I resist the invitation? Come to the warehouse alone or she dies. Although, for future reference, you might want to get someone to spellcheck for you. You spelled dies, come and warehouse wrong."

"No one gives a fuck about my spelling."

"You're quite right no one cares, and in even better news, after today, you won't be writing any more threatening notes."

"Do you think I care about your puny threat? I'm not afraid of you." Gregory lunged while Arik danced back.

"You should be. But then again, this sign of mental deficiency isn't your first. No one messes with my pride."

Still tethered to a chair, Kira found his choice of words odd. So this was about ego? That made no sense and didn't explain why the men battled naked.

Except they weren't men.

Eek.

Before her very disbelieving eyes, skin rippled in a way that was far from natural. Or human.

Both men dropped to their hands and knees as fur sprouted. Their faces contorted, a rictus of pain and of change. The very shape of their skulls changed.

And, no, that couldn't be what she thought it was.

She didn't imagine it. That waving and wobbling thing that grew from their butts was a tail. A dark, thick tail for the black wolf and a golden whipcord tail with a tufted tip for the lion.

Impossible, and yet, unless she dreamed, then rolling around her in an explosion of fur, fangs, and violence were two wild animals.

An honest-to-god werewolf and a… What was the proper term for Arik? Werelion?

This enquiring mind *didn't* want to know. Some knowledge a girl could live without, but she definitely wanted to escape. If only she weren't tied to a freaking chair.

The wolf, with a snarl that showcased way too many teeth, broke free from the lion. He spun and lunged at Kira, the malevolent glint in his eyes enough to steal the scream that sat on the tip of her tongue.

Warm blood sprayed her as Arik hit him, claw-tipped paws ripping into the shaggy fur of the wolf.

Turns out I was closer to the truth than I knew when I called Gregory a dog.

Her hysterical attempt at mirth did not ease the situation. The violence continued unabated, the men in fur tumbling in a wild frenzy of slashing limbs. They couldn't control their impetuous momentum. They rolled in her direction. She couldn't move. Their thrashing frames knocked into the side of the chair and sent it teetering.

Crash. She hit the floor, and something cracked. Her head throbbed, as did the arm and shoulder she landed on, but nothing appeared broken thankfully, except for the chair. Alas, it didn't fare so well.

Which was good news for Kira.

The sudden slack in her ropes meant she could wiggle her arms out. Once they were free, it was only a matter of time before the rest of her followed. She crawled from the debris and, once cleared, went to stand…

Only to get squashed!

A heavy weight hit her in the back, sending her to the floor roughly. She cried out in pain, her chin having hit the concrete along with her knees and hands.

Would this awful nightmare never end?

"Get off me," she squeaked, her chest constricted by the weight pinning her. Struggle as she might, she couldn't dislodge the wolf sitting on her back, his moist, hot breath worrisome where it heated her nape.

Didn't wolves like to bite the throats of their prey?

Not a good thought to have given her situation. She might have peed herself if all her muscles weren't frozen.

A lion roared, at least she assumed it was a lion, that or some other giant cat had joined them in the warehouse. Given she hadn't expected either a wolf or a giant cat in the first place, it wouldn't surprise her.

The furball on her back replied with a low snarl.

"Speak English, would you," she muttered.

To her surprise, Arik did. Then again, it was probably because he'd gone human again, or so it seemed since she could see his bare feet at the edge of her visual periphery.

"Hey, dog breath, I would suggest you let her go."

Huh, would you look at that. Arik let his tongue get away from him. Of course, she might have enjoyed it more if he weren't antagonizing a wild animal with its muzzle poised over her neck.

"Get off her. You and I both know you've lost this battle."

Yeah, buddy, you lost. This time she kept the words to herself. Not because she got any smarter, but more because her mouth was so dry and her lungs so starved for air that she doubted she could manage even a squeak.

The body atop her squirmed and went from digging into her with claws to fingers.

Oh gross. He'd swapped bodies while atop her. The shapeshifting thing was way too freaky.

A hand gripping her by the hair, and Gregory hauled her to her feet.

Ouch.

She grabbed at his hand, trying to loosen it. "Watch the hair." In case she did survive, she'd prefer it to be without a scalped spot.

"Shut up." His little shake brought stinging tears to her eyes as it tugged on her abused strands.

Arik uttered a growly noise of his own. "Let her go."

"But I'm not done with her yet. She's yet to beg me for her life."

"Let her go and maybe you won't die. Killing her at this point won't accomplish anything except ensure your execution is painful and prolonged."

"On the contrary, killing Kira would bring me great pleasure since I know it would devastate you. She's your mate."

"She is."

Again with the whole ownership thing. And

how did Gregory know Arik had claimed her? Had Arik done something to her that made it evident to others? The love bite on her neck tickled as if to prompt her.

Gregory wound his fist tighter, angling her neck back and lowering his face to it. He inhaled before he muttered against her skin, "Do you know I had a plan? I was going to make you watch as I fucked her." He licked her, and Kira shuddered, unable to hide her repugnance.

She noted Arik's fingers tightened into fists at his side. His eyes reflected gold, and even though he was in his man form, there was something primitive about his posture, something animalistic about his demeanor. "You have to know that's not going to happen."

"I know, and it's such a shame I'm going to have to skip that part for phase two. Kill her. Then you." His mouth opened over her neck and hovered, a hesitation on his threat so he could stare and taunt Arik.

Cocky idiot. He misjudged Kira. She wasn't about to let herself die, a helpless victim to a maniac. She waited for her chance and saw it in that moment. Down went her booted foot on his bare one, back went her elbow into his diaphragm, and she butted her head sideways, clocking him in the noggin.

It was enough to distract, enough for him to loosen his grip on her hair and for her to yank free from his grip. Let loose, she stumbled, falling to the floor by the debris of the chair. Her hand closed around one of the broken spindles, and she rolled, bringing it with her in an arc. She swung as Gregory dove at her, vaguely registering Arik's yell but more interested in the thwack the stick made as it connected.

It wasn't enough to render Gregory and his rictus-wrenched face unconscious, but it gave her the seconds she needed for Arik to reach them. He hit Gregory in the side, tossing him off Kira, and pounced atop Gregory as he hit the floor.

Arik didn't waste time. He wrapped his hands around Gregory's neck. "You." *Wham.* "Dared." *Thunk.* "Hurt what is mine." With each word, he rapped her ex's head off the floor.

The violence was intense, and messy. She turned away but sucked in a breath as she heard a sharp crack. She'd seen enough movies to guess what it might mean.

He killed a man.

Killed a murderous psycho, but still…people didn't do that. Except he wasn't a person. *He's a lion. An animal. A predator.*

And she was anything but. What Kira was, though, was a survivor. She got her butt moving.

"Mouse, where do you think you're going?" Arik's nonchalant query held a note of amusement.

"Insane?"

"Not quite yet, so get that sweet ass back over here."

Back to where the body lay in all its gruesome glory? No thank you.

He seemed to grasp the fact that she might not want to converse with him over a corpse because he amended his words with, "Actually, on second thought, stay where you are. I'll come to you."

Come to her for what?

Not knowing what to expect of a world suddenly gone mad gave her the impetus to move. She ran, heading in who knew what direction, instinct not letting her stay still. Running even though she knew she had no chance of escaping him. Not only was he bigger and stronger, Arik wasn't human. Arik was a lion.

"Don't make me chase you, mouse."

"Or what, you'll kill me, too?"

"Maybe kill you with pleasure."

Trust a man to find a way to insert sex at the weirdest times.

Her sudden flight didn't last long, and not because Arik pounced her. She went the wrong way and came against a dead end, no way out ahead of her, crates piled high on either side. She whirled, only to see her retreat blocked by the man who stalked toward her. Despite the feeble light and deep shadows, there was no mistaking his intent, or nudity.

She backed away, one slow sliding step at a time.

"I won't hurt you."

"Says the man who turns into a freaking lion."

"Hey, don't act like you're so surprised. I told you I did."

"But I didn't think you meant it," she said with a fling of her hands.

"Well, now you know. So what?"

"What do you mean, 'so what'? You turn into a lion. You know, big carnivore with giant teeth."

Arik's lips twisted in a wry grin. "Stop complimenting him. He'll get an even fatter head."

That caused her to stumble in her retreat. "You mean that lion you turn into…it's like a separate entity? It hears me?"

"*He*"—his emphasis not hers—"hears and understands just fine. And he's being a furry pain in my ass right now."

"Why?"

"Because he doesn't like that you're scared."

"I'm not scared," she lied, arms hugging her upper body in an attempt to quell the trembling.

"You don't have to fear me. I won't harm you, and neither will your ex. I made sure of that."

He meant his words as reassuring. It didn't quite work or stem a big shudder.

Gregory, a guy she'd dated, a werewolf. *Oh my god, how close did I come to becoming one?* Hold on a second, Gregory hadn't bitten her, but Arik had. "Am I going to turn into a lion now that we've slept together and you bit me?" she blurted out, her fingers running over the sore edge of his mark.

White teeth—*my, how big they are. The better to eat me with?* —flashed as he laughed. "No. You can't catch the shapeshifting gene. It's something you're born with, and even with two shifting parents, that's not a guarantee."

"So I won't turn furry and start chasing rodents?"

"Nope."

Well, that was a relief. "I guess I should thank you for arriving just in time."

"If you want to thank me, get your ass over here." He spread his arms in invitation.

"No thanks. I'm good over here."

"Mouse, you're being stubborn again. We both know you want a hug."

Yeah, she did, but she was trying hard to fight the urge to run to him. Why? *Because he turns furry.* Did she really need another reason to avoid Arik?

But he wasn't a lion right now.

No, he was a very naked man, with a body she still clearly remembered touching, striding toward her with a confident swagger and an erection that had her eyes widening.

"Um, Arik, I really don't think I'm in the mood. Or that this is the time or place to indulge."

"Then we'll go back to my place. I could use a shower first."

"What if I don't want to go there?"

"As my mate, it is your place."

Again with the whole pushy thing. She pushed back. "I don't know if I'm ready to be anyone's mate. That's a lot of commitment and a lot of freaky shit for me to handle in such a little amount of time."

"So how about we just call you my girlfriend for now?"

"Girlfriend?" He just wouldn't give up. And, no, she couldn't resist the flattery. The reminder he wasn't quite a man couldn't douse her attraction and interest in him.

"Yes, my girlfriend. And I'll be your boyfriend. Since you're so keen on getting to know me and all that other jazz, we'll date."

"As in go to the movies? Have dinner? Long walks on beaches?"

"Making out in public places, holding hands, and spending the night in a tangle of naked limbs."

"I thought you didn't date."

"I'll make an exception for you."

The shiver that went through her was one of delight as he piqued her womanly side. "During this dating period, I get to stay at my place."

"Some nights."

"What do you mean?"

"Some nights we'll spend at your place, others at mine. I insist we share. It's only fair."

"Fair? Nothing about you is fair."

"How so?" He finally stepped close enough that she could practically feel the heat rolling off him. She longed to press her hands against the smooth plane of his chest and feel it, feel the thump of his heart, the race of it as she aroused him.

"Because you're like a bag of chips left on the counter. You're just begging for me to nibble."

"Then what are you waiting for? Nibble away, mouse."

"I shouldn't."

He drew her into his arms. "Stop fighting it. This is where you belong."

How right he was. One hug. That was all it took to melt her defenses. So what if he turned into a lion and could kill a man with his bare hands? He'd also braved grave danger to come to her rescue. He met her stubbornness with patience and humor. He let her get in her jabs and then wasn't scared to tease her back. And when he touched her...

The world caught on fire.

As least her whole body did. Every nerve ending came to life. Every sensation became amplified from the firm ownership of his hands on her waist drawing her near, to the prod of his shaft against her lower belly, to the soft sensual slide of his lips on her own.

Her arms twined around his neck, hugging him tight, her mouth opening to the prod of his tongue.

Need burned, and she could have whimpered as he teased her, rubbing himself against her mound so cruelly hidden by her pants.

Didn't he know she wanted more? She mewled against his mouth, ground herself against him, and then froze as an amused voice said, "You do realize you've got an audience?"

Chapter Twenty-one

Arik could have killed Hayder for his interruption. Couldn't he see he was doing something important?

He wasn't just making love to Kira. He was easing her fears. Showing her that, while the lion—*rawr*—was a part of him, he was still a man. Her man.

But did his beta grasp what he was trying to do? Of course not, stupid, cock-blocking jerk. While Arik relinquished his hold on Kira, he did lace his fingers through hers to keep her tethered by his side lest she suddenly decide to take flight again.

She'd dealt with quite a bit in the last few days. Her entire world-view was now skewed. It would take some time and explanation for her to accept all the changes, and to accept him as her mate.

Strolling back to the main area, he was glad to see the body had already been disposed of. Shifter justice was swift. Shifter cleanup even swifter. No one would ever find Gregory's body. He had a crew that would make sure of that.

While he noted Kira peering around, no doubt wondering at the disappearing corpse, he dealt with his lackeys, Hayder and Leo.

"It took you two idiots long enough to get here," he grumbled.

"Was our king of the concrete jungle not able

to deal with one itty-bitty puppy?" Leo arched a brow.

"Not the point. What if he wasn't working alone? What if he was armed? The guy was already breaking all kinds of shifter laws. Who was to say he wouldn't have brought a gun to a fang and fur fight?"

"Oops." Hayder didn't sound the least bit apologetic.

"Um, excuse me, but am I the only one who thinks it's weird that you're chitchatting with Arik here while he's in the buff?" Kira interjected.

Ah, there was the woman he'd come to adore. "Kira, meet my beta, Hayder, and my pride omega, Leo. They're shifters too."

"That doesn't explain this weird nudity thing."

"Well, it's not like we change shapes fully clothed."

"That can get awkward," Hayder added. "A lioness in a G-string is a dangerous sight to see."

"Dangerous how?" Kira dared asked.

"Because the Instagram pic I took of it got me pounced on by a trio of them, and they waxed me from head to toe." Hayder shook his head, in rueful remembrance.

Kira snickered. "I would have used Nair. It lasts longer."

Before Kira could give his cohorts more evil tips on ruining a lion's mane, or a lioness' luxurious fur, he tugged her in the direction of the exit. Just outside was his truck, his clothes tossed onto the driver's seat.

He paused only long enough to put on pants and shoes. He could see Kira gnawing at her lower lip, the pensive mood upon her again. He needed to get her back to…not his place. He'd have to run the gauntlet of too many women there.

He drove them, instead, to her apartment, which took her by surprise. The hour was late, the street quiet, and the silence between them dangerous.

He dared not say anything, and for once, she held her tongue too, until they reached the outside door that led to the stairs up to her apartment. She looked at the lock and then her empty hands. "I don't have my purse or keys."

"Good thing I found them in the alley then." Along with that note. He didn't want to think of what might have happened if Gregory's cocky pride hadn't forced him to leave it.

He pulled her purse from the console box between the front seats.

She unlocked the front door and turned, her mouth opening, probably to speak, but he took advantage and stole her breath with a kiss.

While she might prove uncertain about him and their future, her passionate nature knew what it wanted. It wanted him.

He hoisted her and said, "Wrap your legs around my waist." She complied and giggled into his mouth as he jogged them up the steep flight of stairs.

"I could have climbed them myself," she said at the top as she leaned to insert the key into the lock.

Yeah, she could have, but he'd done it for selfish reasons. One, he got to hold her, and two, when she started panting, he wanted it to be because of him and not those wretched stairs.

They made it into her apartment, and then no farther. He'd meant to stick them both in a hot shower and wash the stink of the wolf from them both. However, alone and with her so eager and delicious, her mouth devouring his with frantic urgency, he forgot his plan.

There was only one thing he needed right now. Her, and the nearest wall.

He let her down, but only long enough to drag her pants down and strip off her top. His trousers also met the floor in a wrinkled pile he'd regret later.

With her naked, just the way he wanted her, he hoisted her again and meshed his lips to hers. Her skin rubbed against his, velvety soft. The erect peaks of her nipples dug into his chest while her moist core honeyed his shaft as it slid back and forth between her thighs, teasing them both.

"I want you," she gasped against his mouth, gyrating her hips and making a sound of desperation.

"You have me," was his reply. For now, and forever.

He sank himself into the glorious heat of her sex, reveling in how she milked him, the muscles of her channel gripping him so deliciously. As he seesawed in and out of her sheath, the cream of her desire coated him and eased his passage.

He could feel her mounting pleasure in the closeness of her uttered mewls, the raggedness of her pants, the digging of her fingers into his back.

The same urgency affected him, and he pounded into her, holding her tight, finally allowing himself to truly believe she'd escaped unscathed.

To think he'd almost lost her, almost lost her to arrogance because he'd rushed to confront the enemy instead of going after her with a plan. But when he'd read the note and knew she was in danger, all rational thought evaporated.

The beast took over the man and went to the rescue—and prevailed. *Rawr.*

Kira was safe. His mate was in his arms, atop his cock and crowning him with orgasmic glory. She cried out his name as she came, her pleasure sweeping through her in shuddering waves, a pleasure he joined. He might have roared as he came. He definitely nuzzled her neck, sucking anew the mark he'd made.

They clung together, two bodies with one fate. One future and…

A meddling mother who pounded at the door and yelled, "Arik Theodore Antoine Castiglione, I know you're in there."

Kira shouted, "Hey, Norma, fancy you showing up," before humming the theme to *Psycho*.

As his mother screamed in rage, Arik laughed. And laughed. Life in the pride was about to get more chaotic. He couldn't wait.

Epilogue

Belonging to a lion's pride took some adjusting. For one, Kira had to learn to live without any expectation of privacy. She now understood why Arik employed the touch screen system, which relied on fingerprint scans and even facial images for security. Even with those measures, his mother found ways to invade their home. Often at the most inopportune moments.

Bang. Bang. Bang

"Why can't any of you use a bloody phone?" Arik roared, one of those times when they'd disturbed his pursuit of the sensitive spot on the nape of her neck.

Kira almost roared a time or two with him. A human roar, of course, because, to her relief, Arik had spoken the truth when he said his whole furry deal wasn't contagious. Still, though, she wasn't reassured by his mention that some of their children would carry the gene.

Children.

Babies.

Big eek!

One of these days, it would happen. Or so he so arrogantly assumed. They'd talked about kids. He was all for having a litter, the sooner, the better. Kira, however, stuck to her guns, insisting that they needed time to get to know one another.

But that conversation had happened a while ago. A few weeks as a matter of fact and much had changed since her initial shocking immersion into his life—and his secret.

For one thing, he wasn't the control freak she'd first accused him of being. Well, he was, just not in the way she initially expected. For example, he was a freak about his space. Arik liked his apartment kept a certain way, to which end he had an army of cleaners come in daily to keep it spotless. It was uncanny how thorough they were.

Kira enjoyed testing them, leaving smudges in odd places and putting dirty dishes under the bed, in the vanity drawer. She even balled up some underwear and stuffed it with other dirty laundry in the freezer.

Wiped clean, washed and put away, laundered and folded in her drawers. It was unnatural how they always knew. Was it crazy to suspect Arik of employing elves instead of real people? He denied it, but she had a feeling. If she could only catch this mysterious cleanup crew at work...

Cleanliness wasn't his only adorable neurosis. Like many felines, Arik liked to nap, in the sun on that giant pillow she'd noticed on her first visit. The quirky part was he enjoyed napping as a man, in the nude.

While coming across a naked hunk, stretching tanned muscles warmed from sunlight, was kind of delicious, it did kind of freak her out the first time since she'd brought her aunt with her to show her that Arik was indeed a real boyfriend with a real condo and that, no, she wasn't lying to avoid a blind date with Auntie's friend Petunia's single, balding, forty-year-old son.

The "oh my" her aunt uttered wasn't entirely due to shock, and the color in her cheeks not just embarrassment. Arik, that naughty feline, just grinned when Kira chastised him for traumatizing her aunt.

Then Kira mauled him for being too utterly delicious. But after that naked incident, she made sure to peek inside before letting any visitors in, and her family stopped all their matchmaking attempts.

As to her initial accusation that he would curtail her freedom and that his misogynist attitude would have her tied to hearth and kitchen? Wrong. He really had only initially kept her closeted out of concern for her safety. With the danger eradicated, she had free rein to come and go as she pleased. She had to make only one concession. If she wasn't with him, then, given her position as his mate, she had to tolerate a bodyguard shadowing her movements when she left the condo.

It was a small price to pay for the utter happiness life with Arik brought her. And besides, she kind of enjoyed the rotating lionesses he assigned to her—because, as it turned out, the pride was mostly women, and they were the true hunters.

A mugger learned that the hard way when Reba made him cry for his mother and promise to do community service.

Life was different, but good. Real good.

I'm happy.

Truly and utterly. Happy with Arik, a man she spent all her spare time with. A man she slept with every night. While they'd initially started out taking turns at each other's apartment, her lack of space, a live-in cook, and the most awesome shower soon put an end to that. But it wasn't his splendid amenities and apartment that kept them together. Kira just enjoyed being with him. The thought of going back to her place, even for one night, without him, didn't appeal at all.

Because I love him.

Huh. I wonder when that happened. She couldn't pinpoint one particular event, but it had happened. She loved a lion.

Peeking at him where he sat perusing the stock market on his phone while chewing on some crisp bacon, she blurted out the momentous news. "I love you."

"I know." Smugly said.

She blinked. "What do you mean you know?"

"Because of the letter A."

"What does A have to do with anything other than being the first letter in your name?"

"Because it also stands for awesome."

"And arrogant."

"Are we back to alphabetizing my attributes? B is for brave."

She laughed. "Don't you dare start again. Besides, there's only one set of four letters that interest me."

"Oh?" he said, putting down his phone and ignoring his meal. "And what might those be?"

"M.I.N.E."

The only word she needed to have him drag her onto his lap for a scorching kiss.

A whispered, "I love you," vibrated against her lips, his softly growled admission fueling her passion.

And after they were done, panting, glowing, and cradled together, ignoring the pounding at the door, she held still as she tried to figure out what she heard.

It should have been impossible. Arik was a lion, and yet he was— "Purring?"

Indeed, he was. *And when an alpha purrs, pleasure is sure to follow.*

*

A few days later…

Babysitting duty. The indignity of it burned. Didn't Arik know that Hayder had better things to do on a Saturday night than babysit Jeoff's baby sister? Important stuff like washing his luxurious mane, or playing the latest Call of Duty with his buds online.

But no, he was *ordered*—and yes he mentally finger quoted—to play bodyguard to some wolf chick as a favor to Jeoff.

He knocked but didn't wait for an answer at the condo door. Being the pride's beta gave him certain liberties, such as access to all the units in the building. He walked in, and stopped dead.

Literally, and with good reason, given a gun wavered in front of his face.

But the weapon wasn't the most shocking thing. It was the possessive growl of his lion and the truth that gobsmacked him when he caught her scent.

Mine.

Uh-oh.

The End…

…of Arik and Kira's story, but the fun continues in A Lion's Pride series with Hayder's story, *When a Beta Roars*. Followed by our 'gentle' giant, Leo, *When an Omega Snaps*.

CPSIA information can be obtained
at www.ICGtesting.com
Printed in the USA
BVHW04s0828090718
521166BV00019B/353/P